These Times

by
Darren Ashworth

Copyright © 2020 Darren Ashworth
All rights reserved.
ISBN: 9798673862995

Dedication

To my wonderful, amazing, and supportive wife Adele. Without her, this book would never have been written. Thank you for the constant support you have always shown me. Thank you for suffering through the pain of reading/re-reading my drafts and your subtlety when you had to tell me they were rubbish.

Thanks to Sharon, who employed me when others wouldn't and kept me writing when I wanted to quit.

Myths of the Forest

The hot midday sun blazed down on the tired sweaty hulk of Thomas. He was bent over and panting heavily, trying to regain any trace of stamina he could. Thomas looked up at the sun and tried to figure out how long he had been on the run. The beat of his heart pounded in his head and all ability to reason seemed hard to grasp. He looked back along the path he had cut through the cornfield and saw a cloud of dust rising above the crest of the last hill. The mercenaries were close and still gaining on him.

He turned back and forced his aching leg muscles to stumble on toward the edge of the forest that loomed a little way ahead. Thomas reckoned he needed to sprint in order to avoid being seen. They would follow his trail easily enough but, in the forest, he could hide and possibly lose them. The mercenaries they hired from Lana were often heavily superstitious and Thomas hoped they wouldn't actually dare to cross into the forest at all. The forest was steeped in myth and folk law. It was also the basis of many horrific urban legends in Lana.

Thomas tried to run towards the treeline but his muscles screamed at him. He was exhausted. Stopping to rest had only let the fatigue catch up with him. Thomas hobbled and half-skipped along, forcing his muscles through the pain. He pictured what would happen if they caught up with him. Thomas visualized the torture he would have to face and imagined the pain he would feel. Fear crept through him and sent surges of adrenaline around his body. He bolted forward, panic temporarily quelling his pain.

After what seemed like an eternity of deafening heartbeats and mind-bending pain, the treeline was finally within reach. Thomas risked a look over his shoulder. There was no sign of his pursuers. Worryingly though, there was also no sign of the dust cloud. They must have crossed into the field.

He turned back and tried to increase his speed. Unfortunately, he had lingered too long in looking over his shoulder and tripped on a rock. He fell forward and landed on the soft dusty earth. With his ear now close to the ground he could hear the distant sound of hooves.

Damn it, he thought, no wonder they had caught up with him so quickly. The Council had obviously spared no expense and issued them with horses. It was rare that such creatures were seen in this valley let alone used to track down runners like him.

Thomas was back on his feet, running as fast as he could. His body screamed at him to stop but his brain would not listen, fear was in the driver's seat now. His vision blurred. He felt sick. He desperately wanted to collapse but knew that being caught would be a hundred times worse than anything he felt now.

Thomas was so busy with his internal battle between mind and body that he hadn't noticed passing into the forest. He stumbled over a thick root and, barely keeping his footing, came to a stop. Thomas looked out over the field he had just crossed. The group was coming to a stop near where he had left the path. He watched nervously as they checked for tracks. One of them had his head close to the ground. He called out and pointed straight at Thomas. He thought they had seen him but then they pointed further along the forest edge. The man on the ground argued with them and pointed at Thomas again. Eventually, they seemed to come to a decision, and seconds later they were back on their horses heading his way. Thomas panicked, he felt he had nothing left in him to keep running.

Just then, he noticed a small grey squirrel sitting on a branch above his head. The squirrel appeared to be waving at him.

Thomas thought then that he might be more exhausted than he had realized, or perhaps he had been out in the sun too long and was very dehydrated. It had been a long journey on foot from his home in Lana. This had to be the reason he was now watching a squirrel wave at him. Even worse, it appeared to be beckoning him up to the branch it sat on. He figured somewhere in his exhausted mind his subconscious was trying to tell him to climb the tree. So, with the little strength, he had left; he hauled himself up to the lowest branch he could find. The tree was old and large, the branches thick and sturdy. He grabbed the next branch and clambered up again. The branches were closely spaced and, even in his tired state, he soon sat alongside the squirrel. The creature hadn't moved but it had now stopped waving at him. Every time Thomas looked at the squirrel it put a claw in front of its mouth and made, what Thomas couldn't quite believe, was a 'shush' sign.

They sat quietly in the tree, some twenty to thirty feet above the ground. It was a few minutes before Thomas heard approaching hoofbeats. The party seemed to have stopped just shy of the forest edge. From all the shuffling and rustling, he imagined they had all dismounted. He heard a couple of voices talking but couldn't make out the words. More voices joined them and as they grew closer, he could hear what they were saying.

"Just get in there you useless prats!" a stern voice said, he sounded like their leader.

"I ain't moving nowhere, if you're in such a hurry to catch im, you go first."

"Look, what are you worried about? Fairy tales and ghost stories?"

"Yes," chorused several voices.

"What? Really?"

"I don't know about ghosts, but I sure do believe in Leshak!"

There were several grunts and mumbles of agreement.

"Leshak? You don't really believe in that do you?"

"I heard stories, enough to make me not want to go in there."
"A shape-shifting Forest Guardian'?" the leader mocked.
"Yeah."
Thomas knew those stories all too well. It was only the fear of being caught that had driven him this far into the forest. Now he feared the legends just as much as they did. Especially as he was sitting next to a curiously helpful squirrel.
"Those are just children's stories told to keep them out of the forest!"
"No, well, yeah. But I also heard it from Billy, my cousin's mate's husband. Says he was gathering firewood, only it was late at night and he couldn't find any dead wood lying on the ground. So, he takes his axe to a young sapling on the edge of the forest. The next morning they find him speared on a branch of the old oak tree back in Lana."
"I remember that! He was there for weeks, wasn't he? No one could un-spear him and there wasn't a soul in Lana that dared to cut the branch down."
"I thought they said that was due to him falling on it?" a new voice added.
"What? How do you fall and spear yourself on a branch growing sideways?"
"I heard he owed Lenny and KneeCaps—"
"Maybe if the wind was in the right direction—"

"Hang on. If Billy was speared then how do you know what he was doing the night before?" asked the leader.
"My cousin told me."
"And who told him?"
"I dunno, it was his mate I guess."
"But I saw Billy in the market square last Saturday!"
"Did ya? Oh, well maybe it wasn't Billy then."
"You don't even know!" the leader said, exasperated with where the conversation had ended up.
"Look, his face was smashed in when I saw it, how was I to know who the hell it was?"
"So you're giving up on your biggest payday this decade, because of some urban legend? Which sounds dubious, to say the least."
"Dubi- what?"
"A load of old crap." clarified the leader.
"I know the pay is huge, but I'd rather have a face and no branch poking through me!"
"You don't know what happened to that body on the tree! Or even who it was!"
"Say what you like, I don't see how anything other than a monster could make a human kebab twenty feet off the ground with nobody noticing."
"But look at it this way, even if there is a monster in there and the stories are true, we'll be fine as long as you don't hurt the trees," reasoned the leader.
"Oh yeah, and what if one of us breaks a branch or twig as we walk through? Suppose we stub our foot on a branch and break off some bark or something?"

"Look, he's getting further away as we speak! Just get in there!"

"Ok, here's the deal. You go in there first an we'll follow, a little distance behind though."

"Right, fine, it's a deal. Goddam idiots."

Thomas heard footsteps approach the edge of the forest and then stop. There was a rustling as if someone was shifting their weight from one foot to the other.

"You know, on second thoughts, the light is beginning to fade—"

"It's midday!"

"But in there you can get lost easily and, before you know it, the sun's set. I have a better idea. Let's camp on the hill up there. We'll post sentries on the North and South and we'll catch him whichever direction he takes."

"We can't guard the whole forest!"

"I don't think we'll need to. If I know Thomas he'll head for the edge of the lake and use it to escape. We'll be able to watch the shoreline from the hill."

Thomas heard the group mumble to each other, then there were sounds of horses being mounted and clomping away. Thomas looked down at the furry squirrel beside him and it made a 'thumbs up' gesture. He wondered about the legends of the forest, about Leshak. What if the squirrel wasn't just his subconscious? What if it was the Forest Guardian? The local lore told tales of travelers being led astray and never being heard from again. Stories of giant trees that stalked the forest, protecting the other trees from harmful intruders. But then again, folk in Lana weren't the most trustworthy sources of information. Only last week he had overheard Wilbert Huffington telling tales of flying saucers and dancing lights in the evening sky. It just so happened that was the same evening he had been found face down in the mud outside Gilford's bar.

He looked around at the nearby trees and down to the forest floor, apart from the flutter of wings and the odd scampering of more squirrels, the forest seemed deserted. He glanced back at the squirrel, but it had vanished.

Hector

Several miles south of Thomas, Hector Winterslow gently dabbed the fever-inflamed brow of his dying wife, Louise. He sat back in the chair beside her bed and tried to get comfortable. He failed miserably and leaned forward again to clasp her hand. It felt cold and clammy; he gave it a loving squeeze but felt no reaction.

This was it, he thought for the twentieth time that day. It must be close now; she couldn't have long. He felt caught in a swirling vortex of emotion, between the bitter down draughts of depression to the final feeling of release. He had ridden this emotional rollercoaster for the last few months and he felt exhausted. He just wanted it to end. For her, for him. But even that thought left him feeling guilty and selfish. How could he wish for his own wife to die?

It ripped him apart to see her rapid deterioration from the kind, loving, free spirit that he married, to the shell she now was. She was a barely conscious husk that spent days fighting for each breath.

Louise took a slightly longer breath and her exhalation rattled. Hector shuffled to the edge of his seat, his heart racing in fear again. She took another breath.

Something had changed, Hector felt it. Louise exhaled another rattle and died. He knew that was it. He didn't know how he knew; he just did. She never took another breath. He started to say goodbye when a lump formed in his throat. Memories of when she first fell sick flooded his mind. Tears formed in the corners of his eyes and as he closed them, the tears flooded down his face.

They were living in the town of Halmington, on the south edge of the lake. Hector was walking along the promenade with Louise. He was experiencing one of those moments in life where everything seemed to be just right. He had a great job, a great home, and a wonderful wife. He affectionately squeezed her hand as she caressed her baby bump. Hector still couldn't quite believe he would be a father in a few short months. Louise smiled back at him and put her arm around him. Together they strolled down the promenade towards the harbour. Louise loved to watch the fishing boats return from their day on the lake.

As they approached the small pier that jutted out into the tranquil water, a dark-cloaked figure loomed into sight in front of them. The air around the figure seemed to be somehow darker than it should have been. It was as if the figure was absorbing any light that came near it. The figure appeared more like a shadow than a person. Yet it was a person, a female from what they could tell. The hood was pulled over her head and it covered her face in shadows. Louise and Hector tried to give the woman a wide berth, but every time they moved away the figure matched it exactly. They were barely a couple of steps away and the woman was heading straight toward Louise. Hector went to stand in between them but the figure hopped forward and barged into Louise. Louise was sent sprawling backward onto the hard ground.

"Hey! What the hell!" Hector yelled at the woman. She continued walking and Hector grabbed her by the arm. As she spun around the hood fell from her head. Her face, revealed in the sunlight, was pretty. Her piercing blue eyes added a much-needed colour to her porcelain skin. She had long, straight black hair that disappeared beneath her cloak. He knew that hair, those eyes, that face.

"Carla?" he said.

She smiled back at him, her eyes piercing into him like a snake targeting its prey.

"Hey, Hector."

He shook himself from the unnerving stare and rushed to help Louise. She seemed shaken but otherwise unharmed.

"Who on Earth is this?" Louise demanded.

"This is Carla. I knew her several years ago."

"Knew? Come on Hector, we were far more than acquaintances."

Louise raised her eyebrows.

"We went out for a couple of years," Hector said.

"Oh."

"You didn't tell her about us?"

Hector scowled at Carla. "I didn't mention you because it was a part of my life I'd rather forget."

"Now, now Hector, it wasn't all bad."

"Come on Louise, I've had enough of this."

"Hector, wait! I'm sorry, it's just been so long, and I've just broken up with Tom."

"You did? Well, I'm sorry to hear that, but it changes nothing."

"It was for the best. Anyway, look at you two! You have a baby on the way!" Carla took a step towards Louise and placed a hand on her stomach. Louise looked uncomfortable at the sudden invasion of space from someone she didn't know. Carla muttered something under her breath as she patted Louise's stomach.

"Erm, thanks," said Louise, uncomfortably backing away.

Hector saw the look on Louise's face and pulled Carla's hand away.

"Thanks Carla, but we really must be going."

"Oh well, good luck then." Her eyes were filled with malice. "And I hope your child is born healthy."

Hector and Louise exchanged worried glances; there was an air to Carla's voice that unnerved them. They turned and hurried away. Several moments later Hector turned back and could still see the dark outline of Carla. She seemed to be watching them hurry away. Hector felt a chill run down his spine. Then, as if a breeze wafted away a cloud of steam, her figure dissipated into the air.

Hector was jolted back to the present by the arrival of a highly stressed nurse. He burst through the door and darted over to the monitors that Louise was plugged into. Looking at the readouts, then glanced over to Hector, and shook his head.

"I'm sorry Mr. Winterslow, she's gone."

"I know, I know," Hector said, lowering his eyes to stare through the bedsheets. He didn't want to start crying again in front of the nurse.

"Even if I'd got here sooner, she wouldn't have—"

"It's okay, we agreed to not resuscitate."

The nurse sighed with relief.

"Oh, I see, I'm sorry for your loss. I'll leave you for a moment but the doctor will have to pop by shortly."

He switched off all the monitoring equipment and went to leave.

"Sure, thank you," Hector said.

"If there's anything I can do, please—"

"Thank you, but I'm fine."

The nurse left and Hector was alone. The silence in the room was deafening. Surprisingly he realised how true his last comment to the nurse was, he was fine. It had been such a torture watching Louise's health degrade, with her innocent mind trapped inside a cursed body. Since the miscarriage of their child, her body had never seemed to recover properly.

Now she was gone it felt like part of him had been ripped away, a swirling vortex in his core around a large void, that felt as if it would never, could never, be filled again.

Life just didn't seem the same anymore and he couldn't even begin to think about how it could be.

Yet a part of him felt an overwhelming sense of relief. She had finally been set free. Her torment was over and she was free of her cage. He looked at her face, despite the tubes and monitoring wires, she looked peaceful, almost happy. He kissed her gently on the forehead and sighed heavily. A releasing sigh that had been years in the making.

"Goodbye beautiful, I'll miss you so much."

A lump formed in his throat and tears welled in his eyes again. He felt the wave of emotion rise in him and, falling back into his seat, he started to cry.

He had no idea how long he had wept, but finally, the door burst open and a battered humanoid robot walked in. Its once sleek metal frame was dented and the paint was peeling from the chest plate.

"Hi, Mr. Winterslow," it said in a strangely chirpy voice. "I'm Doctor Kelpie. I hear your wife is dead."

Squirrels and Deities

Thomas climbed down from the tree as quietly as he could. Although he had heard the posse leave, he couldn't be sure they hadn't left someone on guard nearby. He reached the ground and crept back toward the edge of the forest. Thomas hid behind a large shrub and looked out over the field to the path. Sure enough, one of the mercenaries was setting up camp by the road.

Thomas considered waiting till nightfall then sneaking past him along the bank of the lake. However, the following morning they would find his tracks and he would be in the exact same situation as he was in now. He would be on the run with them biting at his heels. The option he most fancied was to make it to the lake and somehow sail across. But the only problem was the leader had guessed he would do exactly that. So failing that, if he could get back to Lana he could head northwards into the hills. He might even make it to the outlands where they would never dare to follow him.

Thomas slipped back into the forest and headed eastwards towards the lake. The forest was a cool and pleasant change from the baking heat he had just endured. He stopped and reached into his small pack to pull out a canister of water; it was barely half full but he took a long drink. It seemed like with every step he took, the scattered bushes that littered the forest floor grew thicker and thicker till eventually, they covered it completely. He continued and before long he was pushing branches aside and stepping gingerly through thicker patches of thorn bushes. He turned southwards to head deeper into the forest and eventually found a clearer path. It led away from the unkind bushes and into a denser section of trees that lined a track he presumed the forest wildlife had made. The large roots of the trees crossed the path in ridges he had to hop over.

Thomas was trying to head east but the forest seemed to be leading him in a completely different direction. Each time he tried to correct his course it felt like the trees wouldn't let him through. At one point he even tried heading back the way he had come, but the forest seemed to have other ideas and resisted him from doing even that. Tree roots would seem to suddenly jump an inch higher and trip him. Despite the lack of wind, branches would sway wildly in his direction. He started to panic. The forest was pushing him towards its center. Hector's stomach turned at the thought of what was waiting for him there. At that moment, in the forest with little view of the sky and absolutely no idea how he was going to get out of it, he felt like he was losing his mind.

It was at that precise moment the squirrel chose to re-appear. From seemingly nowhere the little fellow popped into existence and hopped along the ground toward him. Thomas backed away from it, fear of the unknown instantly gripping him. Then he laughed and realised how daft he was being, afraid of such a harmless creature as a squirrel. He watched as it brazenly scampered up to within a foot of him where it stopped and sat back on its haunches.

The squirrel waved at him again.

It appeared to be beckoning Thomas to follow him. Thomas was surprised and intrigued at the same time. He wondered if his mind was once again playing tricks on him, yet he followed the little creature anyway.

Thomas followed the scampering fury tail for several minutes, then his mind started to wander. He was heading into the center of the forest again. Thomas turned and was about to flee.

"Hey!" cried a voice over his shoulder. He spun around but the forest seemed deserted, apart from the squirrel who now faced him.

"Thomas, you really need to follow me," the voice floated through the air towards him.

"What? Who's there?" he called out to the forest.

"It's me. I'm Yorik."

Thomas looked down at the squirrel. He could have sworn he just saw its mouth move as those words came out, but surely not, he thought. But then again, this had been an unusual day.

"It's me, I'm the voice you're hearing," said the squirrel, waving again.

"But . . . but—"

"I know it's hard to get your head around this, but it really would save some time if you could skip all the shock and surprise and just accept that I'm a talking squirrel."

"Are you . . . the . . . well . . . Leshak?" Thomas stammered.

"No, I'm not Leshak. Although I do want you to meet her, and she's rather interested to see you."

Thomas panicked and ran away from the squirrel. He had no idea how to escape but he felt he had to. He bolted back up the path only to be tripped in a few strides by an unseen root. Thomas fell to the ground into some thorny bushes that clawed at his clothes. He struggled to pick himself up, but the bushes seemed to be actively pulling him back down. In all his struggling he barely managed to turn his head to look at the squirrel, who was now sitting level with him on the path.

"Look, please come peacefully. It makes our job so much harder if you fight." said the squirrel.

"What do you want with me? I didn't do anything to the forest! I was just trying to get out of it!"

"Relax, Thomas, we know. We know that you were chased here and we know that you mean no harm."

"So? Can you let me go? I'll head straight out of here, I promise."

"It's not that simple, Thomas. You see, we brought you here. We need you to see Leshak."

"Why do you keep saying we?"

The squirrel clicked its fingers together in a way that nature never intended squirrels to do. There was a bright flash and instantly, in front of Thomas, were at least twenty squirrels.

Thomas gingerly untangled himself from the thorny bushes, which had decided to let him go. He stood up and faced the squirrels.

All twenty of them shrieked at him and took a step forward and shrieked again. The sound was hideous; it made him feel like his ears would start bleeding. He slammed his hands over his ears but it didn't help, the noise penetrated deep into his brain. The squirrels took another step towards him and the sound intensified. Thomas couldn't take another second of it. He felt like his head would explode. He ran and ran and they chased closely behind him. Eventually, the noise faded as he gained a little distance. No matter how tired Thomas felt, his legs kept carrying him further away from that monstrous sound. He had absolutely no idea that his legs were carrying him straight into the heart of the forest.

Thomas sprinted through the forest, bounding over the thick tree roots and barging through the undergrowth. His legs ached and once again his head throbbed to the thumping of his heart. He looked back and couldn't see any sign of the squirrels. Thomas slowed to a walk, he panted and gasped for air.

Thomas kept walking even though his whole body screamed at him to stop. The undergrowth slowly gave way to patches of rocky outcrops then large boulders that Thomas had to scramble over. The air felt slightly cooler and there was a dampness to it.

He climbed to the top of a large rock and saw that a small valley opened up below him. It was steep and rocky with a fast running river at the bottom. The water cascaded over the sharp rocks in small waterfalls and foamed over the pebbles and smaller boulders. Further up the river a calm pool had formed in front of one of the waterfalls that was a couple of times Thomas' height. A large old tree had grown roots into the pool and had fallen back against a large outcropping of rock. It looked like an old giant was lying back against a rock as it dangled its feet in the cool clear water.

Thomas headed for the pool and clambered down over the rocks towards the large tree. He approached the pool and looked into its cool clear depths. He stared transfixed by the glistening of multicoloured river-polished pebbles at the bottom of it. After a while he looked up at where he had left the forest and luckily there was no sign of the squirrels. He waited for several minutes, watching the treeline. Eventually he decided they had given up the chase and sat down by the pool's edge. He removed his shoes and sank his feet into the cool refreshing water.

"Thomas, at last we meet." a deep rumbling voice came from behind him.

Thomas spun around and stared up at the large tree that towered over him.

"The one who dares to trespass in my forest?" The voice sounded like the creaking branches of a windswept willow in a very dark wood.

He couldn't quite believe it but the tree had moved from its resting place. Only now did he realise the tree actually had eyes. Well, he guessed they were eyes, but it was hard to tell. They were large knots in the bark that seemed to have no definite center but their depth was like staring into the depths of the night sky. Thomas was almost certain now, that he had lost his mind.

"You're not going mad, Thomas. I am quite real."

Thomas let out a small yelp. He had heard about the legends of Leshak. Now here he was face to face with it.

"You have nothing to fear or worry about." soothed the tree. The tree had sensed his terror and confusion, in fact it seemed to have been amused by reading his thoughts. But then if this was a symptom of losing his mind then it made sense the tree would know everything he thought.

"Really?" Thomas finally managed to say.

"Yes, I would no sooner hurt you than cut a branch from myself."

"So, why did the squirrels drive me here? If not to feed me to you?"

"I'll let them answer that." said Leshak, and he pointed one of his branches over Thomas's head towards the forest.

Thomas followed the direction of the extended branch to the treeline where two squirrels were waving at him. One of them definitely looked like the squirrel who had chased him earlier. At least he didn't have a team of minions with him now though. The two squirrels started heading towards him.

Thomas turned to Leshak. "This isn't all just in my head?"

"No, they are Grace and Yorik. They're trespassers in my forest too. Only I can't seem to get rid of them."

"Why would you want to get rid of them? Don't they belong here too?"

"All living creatures from this planet are welcome here, it's just they aren't."

"They aren't what?" asked Thomas.

"They aren't from Earth—"

"Hey, don't bother Thomas with the details, we can take it from here," said Yorik as both of the squirrels hopped towards Thomas.

"Hiding things from my children! I never agreed to this part of your plan." Said Leshak.

"We don't have access to your immortal enlightenment! But we realise that humans need to learn how to process things in their own time," said Yorik, the smaller squirrel.

"Are you saying you know my children better than I do?"

"Err no! No offense meant either, sorry." groveled Yorik.

"Please don't forget you are guests here." Leshak soothed.

"Erm, indeed," said Grace, the larger grey squirrel.

"We need to talk to you about your wife," Grace said, addressing Thomas.

"Wife?"

"Well, ex-wife. Do you know where she is?"

"Not really, she went North to Suburbia I think."

"Suburbia? Did the retirement team come for her then?"

"No, she just left." said Thomas with a touch of anger.

"Because of your daughter, Eve?"

"So, she said. How do you know all this?"

"Let me ask you this first, how do you know she really went North?"

"She disappeared one day. Left a note saying she wanted to retire, as she couldn't take the loss of Eve." Yorik sighed.

"You don't know for certain then?" said Yorik.

"Well no, I guess not for sure anyway. But she's gone anyway, what does it matter?"

Yorik slapped the pad of his paw to his face.

"Do you know who has been head councilor of Burnim these last few years?"

"No? What's a counselor?"

"For goodness sake, Grace! He's obviously an idiot! Just tell him!"

"Shh Yorik. Thomas, what we're saying is Carla isn't in Suburbia."

"So? Where is she then?"

"Burnim."

"Burnim! What the hell is she doing there?"

"She's a leader there. We believe she might be in trouble."

"What kind of trouble?" asked Thomas.

"We believe she is about to make a big mistake, one that would end the human species."

"What! But how could she have that much power? She only left two years ago!"

"We're not entirely sure of. She has influential friends and we think she has gained the power to control minds."

"Control minds! How did she manage that? I didn't even know that was possible!"

"We're not sure how she did it. We have theories but nothing definite. We must reach the Suburbs as soon as possible."

"What?"

"We need to track Carla down. If we start at the suburbs and look for any rumours of her. I fear we will end up in Burnim though."

"Burnim? Why would we need to go there?"

"To see your daughter again?"

"What?" asked Thomas incredulously.

"We're pretty sure she's still alive."
"Hang on! Who are you? How do I know I'm not dreaming all this?"
"I can assure you we are quite real."
"But why would you help me? And why bring me here?"
"Well, the first is simple; we are an enlightened race who feels it's our mission to help other beings that are under threat. Also, we have taken years, centuries, in fact, to understand your species. We like it, kind of reminds us of our own history when our species was very young."
"Squirrels are more advanced than humans?"
"I think this is best answered by our mutual friend here," said Yorik pointing to Leshak.
"I think we should take a walk Thomas," said the tree. As Leshak took a few strides, the great old tree slowly shifted and morphed. The long wooden limbs shortened and became flesh-like. The deep eyes and knotted trunk around it formed a humanoid face, and the trails of vines became lustrous long hair. In three great strides, the ancient tree had transformed itself into a beautiful woman. Thomas marveled at her beauty. Her hair seemed to shift shades in the wind, from green to blue to red, and every colour in between. It was like watching a waterfall during a fiery sunset. Her eyes glowed a luminous mesmerising green.
She was wearing a long flowing dress that ended just above her bare feet. The grass appeared to be reaching

up to her as if it wanted to be part of the graceful being. It seemed like she was being carried by the Earth, rather than walking upon it.

"Come, Thomas, you are quite safe with me." Her soft, radiant voice floated to him, like the tinkle of wind chimes in a warm summer's breeze.

Thomas sensed there was rather more happening than just speech. He felt his very being reacting to her comforting presence. A wave of power rippled up his spine, instantly relaxing him. He trundled after her as if he were in a waking dream.

"Are you really Leshak? The one the rumours are about in Lana?" he asked, unaware how his relaxed state has loosened his tongue.

Leshak laughed. It was like listening to the sound of rain falling in a forest, or the trickling of water as it poured over the rocks of a waterfall. All with the teeming energy and life of a dawn chorus. Her laughter was all of these things rolled into one, but not a cacophony of sound that confused the brain and hurt the ears. This was a glorious symphony that combined the beauty of them all in a way that overwhelmed the senses.

"Leshak" she said softly, "that is one of many names I have been called, but it is a fraction of what I am. Let's rest in the cavern and I will explain it all." She looked at Thomas and could see concern still clouding his eyes. "As for the incidents in Lana, I take it you mean the body speared on the tree?"

"Erm, yeah," said Thomas. Even in his trance-like state, the idea Leshak was a killer still made him nervous.
"That wasn't me. Despite several influential people in Lana being rather keen on labeling me the perpetrator, I had nothing to do with it."
"But isn't that something you'd say even if you did do it?"
She smiled warmly back at him.
"Would you like me to tell you what actually happened?"
"Yeah, I guess," he answered nervously. Thomas wasn't entirely sure he wanted to hear any of the details. Particularly as he might be about to enter a cave in the middle of the forest with the prime suspect.
Let's say that unknown to most people in Lana, there are two warring factions. A war that started many years ago over a subject that is now as lost as the battles they try to win. These factions have been committing crimes against each other for centuries and have hidden them from the public by blaming such things as natural disasters, accidents, and any wild beasts they can. The only people who know the actual truth are the factions that are sending a message. Well, one day one of the members had the revelation that the war was never going to end. So, he had a not-so-brilliant idea of how to solve it. They would make the other faction, which was considerably more superstitious than they were, believe they had won the favour of a local deity. This is where I was dragged in.

They speared that poor man on the tree and then spread their lies through the town. Before long, the tale of how I killed them was firmly established as local lore."

"What! If that's true then doesn't that make you incredibly angry?"

She laughed again. Thomas loved hearing her laugh. "That is the truth, Thomas. Look into my eyes and see if I'm lying."

Thomas stared into her eyes; they were like infinitely deep whirlpools. He felt many things race through his mind, but there was no trace of deception.

"I have no reason to lie to you. I care not if you think I'm dangerous or here to help. Seeing as the squirrels have asked me to help you, I would rather you be relaxed though."

"Ugh, well, I guess." Thomas still felt on edge, but the effect of her eyes was also very calming.

"Anyway, to answer your question, it doesn't make me angry in the way you think, Tom. It makes me sad to hear my children are lying to each other, for lying is another form of violence. I'm angry that they kill each other so needlessly, and I'm hurt that they use my name to do such things."

"My children?" quoted Thomas.

"Ah, we are nearing the cave. Wait a few moments and I will explain."

In the dream-like state, Thomas had not realised how far they had walked. The river had become deeper and seemed calmer, yet the small movements on the surface hinted at the turbulence below. In front of him the river fell from some way above his head into a deep wide pool. The waterfall was a wondrous mix of thundering raw power and billowing clouds of gentle cooling mist that floated towards him, giving respite from the heat of the sun.

The lady walked along the bank to the rocks that were formed around the waterfall. She sidled along the back wall and disappeared behind the curtain of water. Thomas hung back, not knowing what to do.

"Come, Tom, it's quite safe." her silken voice called over the crashing water.

He followed her and passed behind the water and into darkness.

Fleeing

Hector watched the orderlies wheel his wife from the room and down the corridor to the reclamation center. It would be the last time he ever saw her. They had stopped any kind of funerals or ceremonies after the last catastrophic viral outbreak. Now all bodies were incinerated directly after death.

He already knew what he would do next. Hector had spent the last few years watching his wife slowly die. With little else to do or occupy his mind, he brewed thoughts of revenge against Carla as his hatred and bitterness grew. He was determined to find Carla and make her suffer. His pain for the loss of Louise was determined to be vented.

"Is there anything we can do for you, Mr. Winterslow?" chirped the robotic doctor, abruptly breaking Hector from his vengeful thoughts.

"No, thank you." Hector said looking at the robot, bemused by the cluelessness of its programming and complete lack of empathy.

Hector remembered being part of the crew that first prototyped empathy in robots. The first attempts weren't great and they canned the whole project, the investors could see no profitable value in such skills for robots.

"Mr. Winterslow. Before you can leave your account will need to be settled."
"Account?"
"Yes. It needs settling now your wife is dead."
"Oh, we have insurance, don't we? Surely that's taken care of it?"
"I'm afraid not, Mr. Winterslow. Your insurance has covered the majority of the bills till the time she died. It does not cover disposal and administration costs."
"What disposal and administration costs?"
"The body has to be disposed of and we have certain costs incurred from certifying the death, and environmental taxes, we can provide you with an itemised bill if necessary?"
"But we barely have any money left! I've had no chance to work since Louise fell ill!" cried Hector
"How would you like to pay?"
Hector stared at the insensitive robot; he hadn't realised he was talking as if she were still alive.
"I barely have any money left."
"It's unfortunate about your employment status, Mr. Winterslow. However, you will need to settle your account before you leave."
"And how much is that?" he asked forlornly.
The doctor paused as if he were thinking, then rattled out a stream of numbers whilst Thomas winced.
"That's a lot of money. What happens if I can't pay?"
"There is always a way for you to finance it, or settle it in some other manner."

Hector eyed the battered robot and wondered if it could run, and if so, how fast.

"What if I just left without paying?"

"That situation has already been accounted for. Security was alerted the moment you mentioned you had little money. If you look out into the corridor, you'll see the security drones that will assist in resolving this situation."

Hector peered into the corridor. Just outside the door two spherical battle drones hovered in the air. They were armed with laser cannons and they were pointed directly at him.

"Ah, I see."

"How would you like to pay, Mr. Winterslow?" the Doctor repeated.

"What options do I have?"

"We take debit and credit payments. We can also arrange a payment plan, although you would need to be employed for that."

"Anything else?"

"Our final option is the Internment Reclamation plan."

"Debtors prison!" he scoffed.

"Please sir, that is not a phrase we want to be associated with it. It is merely a means to pay for what is owed."

"How long? When would it start?"

"One moment." The doctor stared straight ahead and seemed momentarily frozen. He finished computing the figure and looked back to Hector.

"Sir, we could assign you to a location tomorrow at midday. You would need to serve five-point-seven-two years in order to clear your debt."

"Five years!"

"Five-point-seven-two."

"Right, six then. Thanks."

"Sorry sir, but we must conclude this quickly, this room is needed already. How are you going to pay?"

"Do I get any time to raise the money? If I can raise it by the end of the month, can I pay then?"

"We will still have to assign you to our debt center, but if you clear your outstanding balance by the time you are due to surrender yourself, then there would be no additional charges and you would be released again."

"Right, well, I guess I better get going then."

"Not quite, sir, you need to follow security to the center for processing."

At that moment the battle robots drifted backwards and a small robot trundled into the room on miniature tank tracks. The robot looked new; it had no damage and the gun metal paint still gleamed. Hector knew that somewhere in that small body a powerful laser was hidden, ready to be deployed in seconds.

"Six two two four nine six, follow me," the squat robot barked at Hector. Its voice was colder and more mechanical sounding than the doctor's. The creators had obviously put more effort into the weapons systems than the human interface.

Hector followed the tank-like robot. Despite its sturdiness the robot moved with surprising agility and speed. It led him down several long corridors and finally into a large dilapidated waiting room.

"Six two two four nine six, take a seat and you will be processed shortly. Do not try to leave without permission or you will be immobilised and taken immediately to prison."

The robot left Hector and returned to a small recess in the wall, resting there along with several others. There were several uncomfortable-looking wooden benches lined up across the room facing a shoulder-high reception desk. Hector couldn't see behind the desk but he presumed another robot was hiding behind it. He took a seat at an empty bench and found that it was even more uncomfortable than it looked.

It was a couple of hours before Hector was ordered into a side room by a bitter, disgruntled humanoid robot that had been cowering behind the large desk. Its faded yellowing paint mirrored its worn out empathy for the human race that it had once been programmed with, ironically it was one of Hector's Beta releases. Inside the room a sniffling administrator looked up at him from behind a large desk, a single screen stood in the middle of it looking like a solitary tree in a vast desert of highly polished wood. The man pointed at a rickety chair opposite him. Hector sat down and as he wobbled on the chair, he noticed it was strategically low enough so his head barely stood above the surface of the desk. He looked up at the administrator perched high on his luxurious leather chair.

"Mr. Hounslow."

"Winterslow."

"What?"

"My name is Winterslow."

"Are you sure?" the administrator said, tapping furiously at his computer. "It says here in your file your name is Hounslow."

"Yes, I'm sure, it's definitely Winterslow. It's been that for years."

The administrator eyed him suspiciously.

"Well, our files are never wrong, I'll have to cross check your claim."

"What?"

"Well, you claim to be Mr. Winterslow, how do I know you're not lying to me?"

"Why would I do that?"

"To get out of paying your bill, of course." The man scowled at him and started prodding at his screen.

Hector noticed a gold embossed name plaque that read Godfrey Winston.

"Are you saying then, that if I can prove I'm Hector Winterslow, I have no bill to pay?"

Godfrey looked at him, the annoyance clouding his face.

"Of course, but you're not though, are you? I just can't seem to find your original file."

Hector reached across the desk and held out his wrist.

"Scan me then, you can surely find me by my identity chip."

Godfrey looked startled, as if it were the last thing that he had expected him to do.

"My identity scanner is broken, budget cuts you know."

Hector withdrew his hand and reached into his coat pocket, he pulled out his citizenship card.

"How about this?"

The administrator snatched the card from his hand and studied it. His eyes opened wide when he obviously reached Hector's surname.

"I see, well, there must be an issue with your admission forms then."

"I wasn't admitted, it was my wife."

"Oh, I see, well, let me check then."

Godfrey resumed his tapping and finally his face lit up, happy he was on familiar territory.

"I see, so you currently owe the hospital this much."

Godfrey turned the screen so Hector could barely peer around it. The monstrous numerical figure that glared back at him turned his stomach.

"That's a lot of money. It seems to have gone up significantly since the doctor told me."

"Really? He should have advised you that the figure he was authorised to quote was merely an indication of the current balance, this is your final settlement. But rest assured, it's very good value if you don't mind me saying. A small price to pay for the health of your wife, I'm sure she'd agree."

"She's dead."

"Oh, yes I see the incineration charges and pollution tax. Well, there's no better place to spend your remaining days than here. So, how do you want to pay?"

"I don't have the money! Can I have some time to raise it?"

"I'm afraid we don't work that way, Mr. Winterslow. We can provide a payment plan but we will require half of your outstanding balance immediately."

"What about our house? Can you use that?"

"According to our records, I see you are already severely in arrears with your payments. If you sold your house you would be lucky to break even, let alone pay our bill."

"Do you have any other options? Surely you can help?"

"The only other option we have is Voluntary Internment. You could work off your debt in, let's see now, erm, seventeen years, three months and two days."

"WHAT!" Hector yelled so loud Godfrey jumped from his seat. Hector saw Godfrey reach a hand under his desk and paused over what he imagined was an alarm.

"Now, now, calm down, Mr. Winterslow. It's not that bad you know."

"The doctor said it would be five, I mean six, years!"

"Ah, did he? Well he shouldn't have. He's not authorised to give payment breakdowns anymore. You see some of the doctor's software is out-of-date and they don't get the latest rates and charges."

"Seventeen years?" Hector asked incredulously.

"Yes, but the good side is that you don't have to pay any rent or feed yourself while you're there, so you actually save money!"

"I don't though, do I? Cause you take it all?"

"Well yes, but at least you aren't paying rent or buying food."

"Is that what all your extra charges are for then?"

"I really think it will help you if you could look on the brighter side of this situation."

"Do I have to go immediately?"

"No, no. We're not monsters, Mr. Winterslow. You have time to gather your belongings and tidy up your affairs, then report to the Debt Reclamation Center when you're ready. There is a time limit though."

"Which is?"

"Erm, midnight tonight."

"What!"

"I can possibly get you an extension, but there would have to be some pretty extenuating circumstances."

"No, that's fine, it's just a lot to process." Hector said, already his mind was boarding a boat and fleeing.

"I understand. Let me process your details and get you all setup. You can pop home and sort everything out."

Godfrey handed him a small card with an address on

it. "If you could make sure you're here by midnight tonight that would be splendid."

Hector stood up and took the card, he shoved it into his pocket and shook hands with Godfrey.

"It's been a pleasure, Hector."

"I wish I could say the same, Godfrey."

"Just call me God."

Hector turned and was halfway to the door.

"Oh, and Hector." Godrefy called to him.

Hector turned back to look at the scrawny human being in his opulent leather chair.

"Yes?"

"Just in case you're thinking of running away, we have the fastest drones in four counties. When they catch you, and they will, you'll be lucky to escape with your life. If you do live, there will be severe penalties added to your bill. You'll be lucky not to die of old-age in the Center."

"I see, thanks for the warning God."

Hector turned and practically ran through the door. He headed for the exit and left the grounds of the ominous grey building as quickly as possible. He ran home and gathered anything of value from his house. After a trip to the nearest pawn-shop he returned home with a pocket full of cash. He gathered the few personal belongings he had left into a bag and left his house once more, this time it would be the last.

Hector hurried down to the harbour and hired the first craft he could find; it was an old wooden canoe. He chucked his belongings into the back of it and climbed aboard. As he rowed away from the dock, he glanced over his shoulder to see the receding town behind him. He would miss it, it was his home. But most of all he would miss Louise. It felt wrong to leave her without an official goodbye or funeral. He knew people thought him old fashioned, but he was shaped by the memories of his childhood, when they buried his Great Grandmother in an actual grave. Even back then it was practically unheard off.

He rowed steadily across the clear, still lake, his paddle and canoe creating the only visible ripples. He steered to the left and headed for the overhanging trees that lined the side of the lake. It was the edge of the ancient forest. He had no intention of entering it. If he hugged the shoreline all the way to the top end of the lake, he might just make it to Lana without being seen. As he paddled, he was suddenly very aware of how unnaturally still the lake was today. There was also a lack of any wildlife, no birds, no fish. He paddled faster.

He soon covered the distance to the treeline and instantly felt safer underneath the lush green branches. He had to occasionally duck to avoid some of the lower ones, but he didn't mind in the slightest, in fact it felt safer to him. For a few moments, as he paddled beneath the trees on the warm summer's day, he almost forgot about the life he was running from. For the briefest of moments, he forgot he was being chased.

He forgot what he had lost, his home, his money, his wife. Sadly, it was very short lived and the reality kicked back at him.

Two spherical drones flew south over the lake at tremendous speed. They hadn't seemed to notice him. He kept paddling, keeping as close to the bank as possible. His arms began to tire and just as he was thinking about taking a short rest, the trees above him thinned till he could see the deep blue sky. A large outcrop of rocks dived from the slopes on his left directly into the clear waters in front of him. The bank and trees faded into the rock, then returned to normal a short distance ahead. He looked up and down the lake, no sign of the drones. Hector took a deep breath and paddled for his dear life.

He was about halfway and feeling like he just might make it, when the sound of the drones returned, heading back up the lake. Hector watched them closely as they approached, but then, the canoe rocked. He looked to the left side and there must have been about fifty water-soaked squirrels perched on the edge of the canoe. They jumped in perfect unison and the canoe rocked more violently in the water. He went to shoo them away but ended up sliding to the left himself. Hector's added weight toppled the canoe and it rolled into the water. Hector was plunged into the fresh cold water, he fought to swim towards what he hoped was the surface. He felt a great number of tiny hands pulling at him, guiding him almost. He burst to the surface and opened his eyes, it was dark. He had surfaced in the middle of the upturned canoe. He grabbed onto the seat above him and rested a moment. It was then a squirrel popped up from below the water. It spluttered then looked at Hector and put a claw in front of its mouth, apparently making a shush gesture. Above Hector and the squirrel, there were nearly fifty damp squirrels dancing on top of the upturned canoe. The two spherical security drones swooped down towards them.

The drones stopped a short distance above them and watched the dancing pack of squirrels. The sight didn't seem to register in their programming, nothing they had observed even compared to what they were now seeing. Then, the final straw, one of the largest squirrels stuck its middle claw up at them. One drone turned to the other and beeped. The other turned to it and did nothing, inside it was wishing it could do the equivalent of a human shrug. The other shook itself from side to side, rolled its optic sensor array and flew off up the lake. The remaining drone tried again to shrug but just ended up rotating on its side. It righted itself and flew back up the lake, chasing after the first.

The Gift

Thomas stood just at the cave entrance looking out through the falling water. He could see where the two squirrels were sitting.
"They will wait for you Thomas," said Leshak.
"It's not that I'm worried about!"
"Oh, what are you worried about then?"
"Why aren't they coming in?"
Leshak chuckled, "This isn't a place for them. This place is sacred. A place reserved for beings that are part of our Earth."
"And they aren't?"
"No, they aren't from here. They have asked me, against my own feelings on the matter, to not tell you their true origin. It will be revealed to you in time, by them."
"Can I trust them?"
"Yes, you can. They have the best interest of your species in their hearts."
Thomas sighed, trying to feel as content as he could with the small amount of information he had.
"What is this place?" he mused, looking into the cave.
"Come Thomas, just a little further and I will tell you everything you need to hear."
Thomas felt confused. There was something about her that made him feel safe. It was like lying on his back in

the middle of a cornfield on a warm summer's day. Through his contact with the ground, he felt connected to something greater. However, his mind was telling him that usually this situation might be incredibly dangerous. He was about to walk into a dark cave with a supernatural being that even magical squirrels were afraid of. It didn't seem good. Yet, there was something about her that emanated a feeling of calm and peace, almost as if she was part of him, or he was part of her.

He followed her into the cave. His eyes quickly adjusted to the dim lighting. It opened out into a large cavern, in the middle of it a narrow beam of light shone down from a small opening in the ceiling. A trickle of water fell from the hole and turned into a fine mist before it hit the cave floor. In the beam of sunlight and immediate vicinity, all manner of fauna seemed to be thriving and reaching toward the ceiling. The walls of the cave were covered in a plethora of mosses and lichens.

"Welcome, to my sanctum Thomas," she said, opening her arms to the cave.

"What is this place?"

"It's a place I have taken refuge, through the troubled times this space has remained constant. This place is protected by very, very old magic."

"Who are you?" Thomas asked slightly nervously, suddenly feeling like he should be very subservient to

the Entity in front of him. "If you don't mind me asking?" he added.
"I have had many names. Leshak, Leshy, Terra, Magna Mata, Earth Mother to name but a few. But I think my favourite is Gaia."
"Gaia?"
"Yes, it was what a race of people called me a long time ago."
"What are you?"
"I promised to answer all your questions and I will. The answer however isn't that simple. I am essentially the Earth. I am the core, the root, the mother of all life that sprang forth on this planet."
"You're . . . God?"
"No, not *the* God you're thinking of. In the early life of the universe and the freshly formed Galaxies, beings of great power roamed the chaos, till the planets slowly formed and each attracted one of these beings. I was drawn to the Earth. I was there when it cooled and became less toxic towards life. I nurtured the creatures that sprang forth from me till eventually a species of sentient beings spread across the surface and slowly transformed it. Many generations died, sometimes they nearly wiped themselves out, yet they survived and prospered again."
"So, you're the Earth?"
"Yes, I think I said that?" she said with a soothing smile.
"But I don't get it I . . . er . . . I don't—"

"Maybe I can help, if I were to show you."
Gaia reached up her arms and they took on a wooden colour. Her hands stretched out and reached towards the ceiling of the cave, each finger turning into slender branches that intertwined elegantly upwards. Her legs and feet seemed to merge with the cave floor and turn into rugged sections of limestone. Gaia's eyes turned lava orange. As Thomas looked into them he felt the overwhelming heat radiating back at him. The heat was so intense he had to turn away.

As he did, he saw the cave was no longer dark and filled with moss. Instead it had become the center of a great green forest. There were no walls or ceiling, just great towering trees that surrounded him on all sides. All around him the forest sang with the essence of life. He felt something touch his head. Gaia had grown another branch and it was curling around his head.

"Relax Tom, I just want to show you where humans enter this picture."

As her branches settled on his head, his mind spun with fresh images. There was a great fiery land, filled with erupting volcanoes and seas of lava. Time flew by very quickly, Thomas had no idea how long it was, but the way the land shifted and changed so rapidly he was guessing thousands of years were passing by in the blink of an eye.

After a while of rapidly changing landscapes and the appearance of seas and lakes. A land he recognised began to form. Giant trees sprang up and the land was filled with greenery. All manner of creatures roamed about in a blur he could barely detect. All of a sudden, the passage of time slowed. He could hear the creatures all around him, he could see them quite clearly. In front of him there was a group of what seemed like apes, but they were like no others he had seen before.

"The creatures before you are the first of a species that will later be known as Homo sapiens. Well, I say first, but they have actually been evolving into this form for many, many years. But, if you take the point of what your scholars classify a human to be, this would be the moment they start to tick all those boxes."

"Humans? They're humans?"

"Yes. They're one of my fondest creations too, and ironically the ones that cause me the most harm."

"I don't understand, what are you showing me this for?"

"I'm trying to show you just how much a part of this world, this planet, me, that you actually are."

"You mean you created us?"

"I can't take all the credit, but you could say I'm your Mother."

"Oh. But that still doesn't—"

"Wait Tom, just watch and listen, it will become clear."

The cave walls were then transformed into a series of brief snippets, or so he could tell. Flashes of humans, now in the form he recognised, building great stone structures. Then there were fields of them fighting each other and then the crumbling of the structures. This pattern kept repeating, although each time they became better at building and better at destruction too. There were all manner of things, from flying machines to towering structures that seemed to touch the sky. Massive explosions ripped those same structures apart as if they were nothing more than a clump of cotton.The scenes stopped once more when everywhere he looked, great towers made of a material he had never seen before, surrounded him. He didn't know how he knew, but he knew they covered the entire surface of the Earth.

"This was a peculiar time for humans and the Earth," Gaia said. "It was the peak of human civilisation. You had reached for the stars and were capable of creations nearly matching the Gods themselves. Yet, you had polluted the very air that kept you alive. You had taken so much from the Earth and left little in return. The creatures I had created and nurtured all those years were being eradicated by your actions and worst of all, you were killing yourselves. This was the first time I had to actively intervene for a very long time. I colluded with Aether and even though it was murdering our own children; we turned on you and drove you back. We made the air you breathed and the land you walked on turn against you. Many, many lives were lost. When it was finished there were patches of civilisation like you see now, but humanity lost many centuries of progress and returned to primitive towns and villages. Burnim and Lana are classic examples of the types that remain and the differences between fractured parts of society."

"How long ago did all this happen?"

"About five hundred years, I mourned the loss of life for four centuries. But I was roused by The Arrival."

"The Arrival?"

"I'm afraid I forgot to mention; whilst I wish to leave no question unanswered, there are some I have agreed with Yorik and Grace not to answer, for the sake of their task at hand."

"What task is that?"

"You must find your daughter Tom. They are here to help you do that."

"Eve! But she's dead?"

"No, she isn't Tom. You have been hideously deceived. She is alive and well, and in Burnim."

"What!"

Thomas felt anger, confusion, and disbelief all rising in him at once. Gaia adjusted the hold on his head and it all seemed to fall away as fast as it had built.

"Calm down Tom, you will find all the answers you seek and more, just relax. I have a gift to give you."

"What is it?" said Thomas dreamily. Her words were loaded with that now familiar trance-inducing lilt.

"It is the ability to change into whatever you want to be."

"Wha—!"

"Relax, I'm afraid this will hurt, but sadly there is nothing I can do about that."

Thomas screamed as if every cell of his body was being ripped apart and reassembled, which was in fact, exactly what was happening to him.

Thomas finally stopped screaming and fell limp in Gaia's branches. She lowered him gently to the floor. As she did the floor grew upwards with vines and leafy bushes to support Thomas's body. Gaia lowered him onto the green leafy bed as it wrapped snugly around him.

She stood up and strode out the cave towards where the squirrels sat arguing.

"But why did you have to taunt the drones? They'll only see that and come looking again!" said Grace.

"Oh, for goodness sake, they only review the videos that the drones flag as suspicious," replied Yorik.

"And you don't think a bunch of squirrels giving a drone the finger would be classified as suspicious?"

"Not rea—"

"I'm sorry to interrupt this fascinating discussion, but I have just given Thomas his ability. When might I be expecting Hector?"

"He should be here any minute, I think. We're just by the lake now."

"Tell me, do the other parts of yourselves argue as much as you two do?"

"Sometimes more," grumbled Grace.

"Yep, and that's because this idiot can't multitask!"

"I can multitask you fur-brained half-wit. It's seeing through six pairs of eyes at once that I can't handle." Gaia sighed and walked back into the cave to check on Thomas.

The Gift*2

Hector stumbled and splashed his way out of the shingle-shored lake. The heat of the day made the air seem stifling. Yet the lake was still ice cold; fed by snowmelt streams from the mountains all around it. Hector shivered and spluttered onto the bank, never once letting go of his canoe. He watched the collection of squirrels closely as they sat further up the bank. All of them were staring directly at him. Any sign of them going for his canoe and he would be off across the lake, he thought, paddling for his dear life.

One of the many squirrels hopped over to Hector. He automatically flinched and took a step back, clutching his canoe.

"Hi Hector. I'm Grace."

Hector stared at Grace, trying to convince himself he hadn't just heard a squirrel talking to him. It had been a very weird morning and he feared he might be losing his marbles.

Grace noticed the thoughts in Hector's mind, and inwardly chuckled at the similarities between her conversation with Hector, and the conversation the other part of her consciousness had with Thomas earlier.

"You're not imagining things, I am real and the other squirrels really are talking to you," said Grace, she turned to Yorik. "What is it with humans and their complete failure to believe their senses when they are shown something unexpected?"

"Generations of conditioning, the unexpected is uncontrollable and therefore labeled as bad. Even if it's the very thing that might save them." replied the now solitary squirrel on the shore, it was another part of the Yorik consciousness.

Hector couldn't believe all but two of the other squirrels had magically vanished. This made him more nervous, where had all the little buggers gone!

"Don't worry, we don't want your canoe. We just tipped you so the drones wouldn't see you and alert the search parties."

"Eh? Thanks I guess. But why?"

"We want to help you. In return for our help, we need you to do something for us too."

"Like what?"

"Like helping a man find his daughter again."

"Oh, I guess I couldn't say no to that, but I am kind of busy trying to escape."

"We can help you there, we'll help you avoid the search parties and clear your debt."

"Erm, how do you know about my deb—"

"We'll explain exactly what, who's, and why's when we reach Thomas. He'll have many of the same questions I imagine, so we can explain it to you together," answered Grace.

"Erm? Thomas?"

"The man we're helping with his daughter." explained Grace.

"Oh."

"Fantastic, well, follow us then, he's in a cave up this way."

Hector pondered whether he was dreaming, maybe it's why he felt surprisingly calm. He felt something in him persuade his mind to let go and follow them.

"Don't worry, we're not going to do anything to you!" soothed Grace, seemingly reading his mind.

"If this is real then you're a talking squirrel telling me to come into the haunted forest. If you're just my imagination, then I've got severe problems." Hector pondered.

Yorik slapped his paw across his face, although the fur lessened the effect. He clicked his claws and Hector was lifted off the ground and spun in the air till he was dangling by his feet. Yorik made some gesticulation and he swung lower, his face level with the squirrels, albeit inverted.

"Listen Hector. If we wanted to hurt you, rest assured, we would have done it by now. We could atomize you instantly. However, we have absolutely no wish to piss about inviting you back to a cave to do what we could do here. And we aren't just figments of your imagination! Got it?"

Hector nodded sheepishly, in an upside-down kind of way.

"Fantastic. Now let's move on, we're already late."

Yorik gently turned Hector the right way up and lowered him to the ground.

The squirrels led Hector up along the treeline until they came to a river where they turned into the forest. It was a narrow rocky path that wound up into the forest alongside the river. They followed the path for some time until, just when Hector was about to stop, Grace and Yorik stopped and pointed across the water. On the other side of the swiftly running river, two small furry creatures were seated on a small rock. They were sitting gazing at a waterfall a little way from them. Although Hector couldn't exactly see them clearly, the creatures were squirrels too. They seemed to be very similar to the ones that were leading him now.

"Here we are," said Grace.

"We just need to pop over this river, those creatures over there, they're kinda with us."

Hector looked down at the water from the small rocky bank they were on. Before them the river was narrower, to the point he could almost jump across. However, the water in front of him seemed quite deep and the surface had strange eddies that hinted at the turbulent currents below.

"So how are we going to —"

Yorik flung himself over the water and landed gracefully on the other side.

"C'mon Hector, it'll be ok, you can make this jump," said Grace. She then hopped over the gap as if she were avoiding a puddle.

Hector looked down at the water, then backed up a few paces and readied himself to run.

Across the river Grace and Yorik bounded up to the two creatures who were in fact, Grace and Yorik.

"Hey," said the newly arrived Yorik.

"You're late," said the Yorik seated on the stone.

"I know, you know I know! We're the same mind!" said the newly arrived Yorik.

"I know! You don't have to explain that to me! I'm you! Remember?"

"Guys, please," said Grace on the rock.

"Why are you arguing with yourself?" asked the alternate Grace.

"He started it," the Yoriks chorused pointing at each other.

Both Grace's sighed.

Across the river, Hector had just built up enough courage to overcome the fear of the turbulent water. He took a deep breath in and started running. His right foot reached the edge of the bank and he was about to transfer his weight to spring across the river.,

"PENGUIN!" yelled one of the Yoriks.

For Hector, it was one of those seconds that seemed to stretch out in slow motion. He automatically turned to see if there actually was a penguin behind him. Whilst

Hector looked behind him, his foot slipped and he fell unceremoniously into the river. After a great deal of splashing, Hector stood up. The water barely reached his waist. As he struggled against the swift current of the river, the sounds of laughing squirrels were deafening.

Gaia emerged from the cave and gave Hector a confused smile.

"What is going on out here?" she said.

Hector looked up to the mesmerising beauty of Gaia, though he had fallen in love with the voice alone. It was so soft, warm, and comforting, yet incredibly powerful. But he couldn't even comprehend how stunning she was. With hair that danced in the sunlight and seemed to reflect every colour in the rainbow and perfectly formed features, she took his breath away.

Hector waded across the river and clambered up the bank. As he stood there soggy and dripping, he stared at Gaia like it was the first time he'd seen a sunrise.

"Hello Hector. Are you alright? If you come with me you can dry off in the cave."

Hector stood there completely motionless, his brain forgetting how to make him speak.

"Hi," she repeated sweetly.

Hector mumbled an incomprehensible reply as he continued to stare dreamily at Gaia. She looked at him as if he had just hit his head on the rocks in the river.

"Well Hector, let's get you inside to dry off." she said smiling. She looked at the four squirrels, still chuckling. "Really you pair! Haven't you got more important things to do than play tricks on poor Hector here?"

"Not until you sort those two out for us we don't," replied Yorik, lounging on the rock.

"I see, well, if you had brought him here on time it would have been over by now. It's dangerous to keep humans in a trance, such as the one I've had to leave poor Thomas in."

"Well get on with it then!" joked Hector's version of Yorik.

Gaia didn't appreciate the humour; she thought the squirrels were getting a little uppity as it was.

"Why are you two still in separate bodies? Isn't it time you re-joined yourselves?" Her voice, whilst still pleasant, held an edge to it. An edge that was cold as ice and sharper than a knife.

"We were, er —"

"Just enjoying the company," finished Yorik.

"Put yourselves back together," she commanded.

"Listen Gaia, no disrespect but —"

"NOW!" She snapped her fingers and the two Yoriks flew towards each other and melded into a squirrel that looked exactly the same apart from being nearly waist high. The two Graces were flung together and coalesced, also ending up waist-high.

"Wasn't that fun!" Gaia asked rhetorically.

The squirrels nodded and hung their heads.

"Hector, come along, let's get you cleaned up." The fierceness had left her voice as quickly as it had entered.

Hector trundled along after her, still mesmerized by such a wonderful being as Gaia.

Inside the cave, Hector saw a resting figure lying on a bed that seemed to have been grown from the cave floor.

"Who—"

"Don't worry about him Hector, you two will meet soon enough. Now I need you to clear your mind. I have a gift for you." Her arms once more turned to branches and reached out green shoots towards Hector.

"But what the—"

"Relax," she purred as her tendrils reached him and curled around his head. "I'm afraid this may hurt; I do so wish it didn't."

Outside the cave the two squirrels nursed their egos.

"I think that was out of order," said the solitary Yorik.

"I know, we were only messing around. We would have melded back together eventually."

"Exactly. Besides, I think she has damaged me, you know. I'm not sure I can split anymore."

"Hmm, it does feel like we've been rammed back together again, I'm just grateful she didn't—"

A blood curdling cry erupted from within the cave.

"So that's Hector sorted then!" said Grace.

Hector was in a very deep sleep. His dreams were particularly vivid and strange. In one he was walking on the surface of a small world, so small that in one complete breath he could walk completely around it. The sphere was divided equally in two, one side was purest white light, the other pitch black. As he inhaled, he felt compelled to walk forward into the white side. Everything was pure, perfect, and peaceful. He felt his lungs fill to capacity as he was midway through the light side. As he exhaled, he was compelled to keep walking and he quickly reached the darkness. He crossed over into it midway through breathing out. It was terrifying. In the pitch black he could sense evil, malicious shapes eyeing him with hatred. Hector was scared, he panicked and gasped for air. The light side quickly approached again and he passed into it. He felt the dark monsters chomping at his heels as he crossed the line.

Each time he breathed in and out he would repeat this cycle. Eventually he realised that this cycle was his life, his soul, his being. He consisted of both light and dark. Purity and evil. There were times his mind and actions were kind, pure, and good. Other times he was overtaken by bad thoughts and actions; these were the ones he fought hard to subdue. Sometimes though he ended up doing them or at least thinking about doing them.

Then he had a moment of enlightenment, an awakening. No matter how much he hated it, he was

made of both sides and he wouldn't be who he was without them. In fact, everybody was probably like this to some extent. The amount they are ruled by either side dictated what type of person they would be.
Gaia was showing him he needed to accept the dark side as much as the light. As he tried to accept it, his panic over being on the dark side subsided. The anger of his dark monsters started to die away too. It almost seemed like they started to respect him as he no longer feared them. Each breath became easier and more relaxed. Slowly, with each traverse of the world, it felt more like a gentle stroll.
In Thomas's dream, he faced a shimmering purple vortex. Thomas felt drawn to it and jumped through. After the swirling purple vortex dissipated, he found himself at the bottom of a large body of water. However, he could still breathe normally. He tried swimming towards what he hoped was the surface. With each stroke, he felt a gentle pull upwards and it increased as he swam. The water around him was dark but punctuated with flecks of incandescent light that moved as if it were alive. As he approached the surface, the water became lighter and clearer till he could see ripples above him. A few feet from the surface he glanced back down into the dark depths below him. Everything looked dark and cold. Something silver flashed on the edge of his vision. Thomas tried to peer into the murky gloom but he couldn't see anything. Then, it appeared. A very large

shark-shaped object swam into the edge of his vision then out again. It was playing with him! He panicked and raced to the surface, three strokes more, two, one. He erupted through the choppy waters and awoke. Thomas sat up on the comfortable bed of what seemed like vines and tree branches. He looked around the cave. Gaia stood in the beam of sunlight and smiled warmly back at him. Alongside his bed there was another, just like his. On this bed there was a man lying down, he appeared to be in a deep sleep. Thomas swung his legs over the side of the bed and stood up, he felt unsteady on his feet.

"You should take things easy, Tom; your body has just taken quite an onslaught."

"What did you do?"

"As I said, I gave you a great gift. One that humans weren't destined to get for another thousand years. Once Hector wakes up, I will explain it."

"Hector? He's Hector?" said Thomas pointing to the body in the bed.

"Yes, he's like you, and he'll be helping you get Eve back."

Almost on cue, Hector opened his eyes.

After some awkward introductions and lots of questions, Hector, Thomas, Gaia, and the two squirrels sat on a collection of rocks by the waterfall. The afternoon sun continued to bake the open stretches of ground. Hector and Thomas were dangling their legs in the cool river.

"So, what now then?" asked Hector.

"You head to Burnim," answered Gaia.

"Burnim? Why? What's there?"

"My daughter," said Thomas dreamily.

"Your daughter? How come she's there and you're all the way out here?"

"I thought she was dead. But to be honest, I don't really know. I need to find my ex-wife and get to the bottom of it all."

"Oh."

"It's because of her these squirrels tracked me down, my wife that is, not my daughter."

"Right," said Hector, trying desperately to understand.

"Apparently that was why they gave me the power to change my appearance and you the power to, what was it again?"

"Tele-something," replied Hector.

"Telepathy," added Gaia. "It's the ability to communicate with your mind, and to read them, with practice."

"Right, telepathy. How do I do that then?"

"The squirrels will teach you, as you travel to Burnim."

"But why do I have to go there? I mean, you seem like a nice enough bloke and all, but I have my own problems."

"If helping another human find his daughter is not a good enough motivation, how about if we solve your debt problem?" answered Yorik.

"Really, you could do that?"

"Yes, and the drones that chase you, we can erase your record," continued Grace.

"You mean I could go home?"

"If we make it through this and you still want to, of course you can."

"Well, I guess it beats hiding from drones by myself."

"Excellent, you have an agreement and your party is formed. I think it's time you started on your journey. I suggest you cross the lake at night. The drones won't be chasing Hector then. He's not that much of a priority criminal; they won't risk damaging them."

"Are you not coming with us?" asked Thomas.

"I'm afraid not, Tom. I have already meddled more in the affairs of humans than I have for centuries. I think I have interfered enough; the rest is down to you. Take the gifts I have given you and drive back the threat that hangs over our planet, that hangs over me."

Squirrel Impressions

Thomas stumbled through the forest, in front of him the squirrels leapt naturally through the undergrowth. His mind was awash with the experience he had just been through. Back in the cave, when Gaia had laid her branch-like hand on his head, his mind had exploded with the experiences of his whole life. Some good, some bad. The rush was unbearable and he hadn't even realised he was screaming out. It was the bad, painful memories that he couldn't bear. All the times he had hurt someone, all the times he had done something embarrassing and all of the parts of his life in-between that he'd tried daily to forget. However, the most painful of all was the death of his daughter.
The experience brought the memories back to his mind as if they had happened yesterday, clear and raw with emotion. Eve was barely six years old when it happened. He had been working at a nearby farm and after a pretty normal day, he had headed home. He and Carla had a house on the shore of the lake that had a small jetty. He remembered how Eve loved to dangle her legs off it and kick her feet in the cool calm waters. The one thing that always confused him was that Eve had grown up living by water, she could swim nearly as well as he could. She knew the dangers of the icy cold lake all too well. Yet when he returned home, Carla was crying hysterically. She told him she couldn't find Eve anywhere. The last she knew Eve

had been swimming around the jetty. At that moment he felt the bottom drop out of his world.

They searched everywhere for signs of her. The local sheriffs were called and as day turned into night, he had descended into a nightmare. Search parties were organised but found no trace of her. Days passed into weeks and weeks into months. Eventually they officially stopped looking and declared her missing, presumed dead. However, even when the empty coffin was lowered into the ground at the cemetery on the hill, Thomas felt no closure whatsoever.

That was the beginning of the end for Thomas and Carla's relationship. When the sound of crying didn't fill the house, they were arguing. Soon they couldn't stand to be in the same room as each other. One day he had arrived home and the place was deserted. Carla had taken everything and left without even a note. He realised how bad things must have been for them when he didn't even care that she had gone, in fact he was relieved. For all he knew she could have been kidnapped, murdered, or just staying with friends.

A few years later he heard rumours that she had taken early retirement and gone North to the Suburbs. However, after the things Yorik had said, he doubted how much truth was in the rumours.

Thomas returned from his memories and realised he had been following behind the squirrels without paying attention to where they were leading him. As he watched them scamper and scurry along, he found his thoughts lingered on what they actually were. From the outside they looked like perfectly normal squirrels but yet they were something else, something much, much more. He chuckled to himself as he saw their great bushy tails undulating along behind them, when suddenly, POP.

Thomas found himself looking at the world from much lower down. He looked down at his body and tried to scream, but his vocal cords wouldn't work. From head to toe he was covered in grey fur. He tried to scream again, this time finding his voice box, he succeeded but not as he planned.

"Squuuuuuuueeeeeeeeeaaaaaak!"

Yorik and Grace turned around and scampered back to the source of the noise. They stopped on a small fallen log and looked down at the furry creature below them. Yorik smirked.

"Thomas?" Yorik asked.

"Squuuueak!"

"Why on earth were you thinking about squirrels?" asked Grace.

Yorik stared at Grace and tried to roll his beady eyes. Hector gestured at Yorik and Grace, trying to highlight the obvious squirrel connection.

"Ah, of course." relaised Yorik.

"SQUEAAAAK!" Thomas cried.

"Ok, Ok, calm down. We should have taught you to control your new powers, but there wasn't time. Gaia gave you the gift of shape shifting, it basically means

that whatever you think of, if you think about it hard enough, you'll change into. You'll be able to control it eventually."
Thomas squeaked manically, his eyes bulging in panic. "Calm down! You'll be fine, you'll always return to your true self. It's like a default setting, it'll always come back. Just clear your mind, try to empty it of any thoughts."
Thomas, despite the sheer terror he felt running through his mind at his furry being, was trying to ignore the strange sensations his new form was bombarding him with. He slowly cleared his mind of thoughts, thinking of nothing but an empty white canvas. Occasionally random thoughts would barge in, as difficult as it was, he let them pass through him. Finally, after a few minutes, there was another satisfying Pop.
"Thomas! You're back!" Grace chirped.
Thomas looked down and sure enough, his old form had returned. Hands, legs, feet, oh how much he had missed being human in such a short time.
"Just try not to think of anything. At all," said Yorik.
"Easier said than done!"
"Don't worry about it, look we've nearly reached the lake," said Grace.
"How come I still have clothes? Surely they would have fallen off when I . . ."
"I'm afraid the answer to that is a little complicated, rather than just changing your physical—"

"I don't know why you're bothering; he won't get it." Yorik interrupted.

"Shush Yorik. It's to do with the way your power works. It doesn't just change your body's appearance; it shifts atoms and molecules around into the form it needs. This includes any clothing, fur, dirt etc. that your current appearance consists of."

"Oh," said Thomas, half understanding what the squirrel meant.

Hector shook his head, as if trying to clear the memories of a bad dream.

"But what about my power then? Am I going to suddenly find myself wandering around like a forest creature?"

"Oh no, not you Hector," replied Yorik matter-of-factly.

Grace sensed the confusion.

"You have a very different gift Hector, yours will take time to develop and you won't get things like that happening."

"Well, you might, but it will be different. Your form won't change but you can project whatever image you want into others minds, so it's similar, but different." expanded Yorik unhelpfully.

"Erm." Said Hector, his face a wall of confused muscles, "What is it then? That I have?"

"It's probably better if you find out when you can start to feel things change, otherwise it'll just seem like nonsense." said Grace.

"But what is it?" Hector cried.

"It manifests in people differently, but essentially you have the power of the mind unlocked."

"The power of the mind?"

"Yes, for some they can walk in other people's dreams, for others it might be empathy to the level you feel what they do. Others still have the ability to read minds, even control them."

"Really? Will I be able to do that?"

"We won't know until your mind adapts to the abilities it's just been given. Maybe one of them, maybe all of them."

"Oh. When will I—"

"Have patience Hector, this stuff will come in time."

They followed the squirrels along the path and the trees started to thin. The mixture of solid rock and patches of earth beneath him slowly gave way to soil then to gravel and pebbles. Finally, the trees fell away completely and they found themselves on a long narrow beach.

Thomas felt like he was losing his mind. Between talking squirrels, talking trees that were actually ancient deities that granted him magical powers, and finally turning into a squirrel. It was just too much. He walked to a small boulder and sat down on it. He stared out into the lake and began to massage his temples, hoping it might drive a moment of sanity into his brain.

Sailing by Moonlight

Thomas and Hector sat looking out at the lake with their backs against a tree. As they waited for sunset all the inane pleasantries had been exhausted. They were now left with either uncomfortable probing questions, or silence.

"What's your story then?" Thomas asked, fearing the awkward pause in conversation.

"Story?"

"Yeah, how come you ran rather than pay the debt?"

"They wanted me to pay the bill immediately, or go to debtors' prison."

"Arseholes! So where's your wife then?" Thomas realised what the answer would be the moment he said it. He cringed in anticipation.

"She died this morning."

"I'm sorry, I—"

"Don't be. It had been coming for a long time. I feel, well, kind of numb."

A pair of drones broke the silence and raced back up the lake scanning for Hector. Hector and Thomas subconsciously pressed themselves against the trees, hoping the canopy and the shadows it cast would hide them. They remained still and watched till the drones disappeared from sight.

"Exactly how much do you owe them?" asked Thomas, returning to his relaxed slouch.

"A lot for one person. Would buy a very nice house in Halmington outright with change. Could probably buy half of Lana."

"So why are they hunting you? Surely, they must be spending more time and money chasing you than they'd ever get back, even with forced labour?"

"It's the principle, and the message it sends. Everyone fears them because of things like this."

"But didn't you know this would happen then?"

Hector sighed. "I guess I did, I just didn't want to think about it."

"There was no way out?"

"No. Running was my only option. Maybe it would have been better if I'd left before she died. But I just couldn't leave her, even though she probably didn't even know I was there, I just couldn't."

"No, I guess not, I doubt I would have done anything different." Thomas patted Hector's shoulder as soothingly as he could. "What do you know about them?" Thomas said gesturing to the two squirrels that seemed to be arguing a little way up the beach.

"Nothing really. They saved me from getting caught by the drones. Even if they nearly drowned me in the process. You?"

"Nothing much, they scared the crap out of me and chased me into the forest where we met."

"Scared you?"

"They may look furry but when you have a dozen of the buggers chasing you."

Hector laughed.

"I guess. What do you make of Gaia hinting they're from another world?"

"Well, at this point, after the day I've had so far, I'd believe anything."

"Makes you wonder what they want though, doesn't it?"

"Hmm."

"It was a shame Gaia couldn't come with us."

"I think she is, she's kinda everything on this planet so I—"

"And you'd be quite right Thomas," said Gaia, who appeared from the trees behind them.

Thomas and Hector jumped up, clutching at their chests.

"You need to be more alert when you get nearer Burnim you know!" said Gaia.

"But you could have at least given us a warning!"

"Or pop up in front of us, that's an option," added Hector.

"I'm here now, just be grateful for that."

There was something about her voice that made Hector and Thomas feel like they should kneel before her.

"Erm, of course, thanks," replied Thomas.

"What do you need from me?"

"What?"

"I take it there was a reason you wanted me here?"

"Oh, I guess it was just the reassurance of having you arou—"

"I have a question," blurted Thomas.

"Yes?"

"Where should we go? Is there a better path to Burnim we should be following?"

"I can't direct you every step of the way, that is not how things work. I can guide you to the place you need to be. How you get there and what you do when you are there, that is for you to live."

"Why?"

"Free will. It is one of the most powerful, and dangerous, gifts you have. You are not bound by fate, well not in a way that is evident to humans. If you were always supplied with the answers, you would never learn and grow."

"Oh."

"So, what information can you give us?"

Gaia sighed; it was like listening to the wind rustling through the trees.

"If I was in your situation I would probably head to Lana, spend the night there, and then head North in the morning."

"Lana? They're still looking for me," cried Thomas.

"They are, but the people looking for you are now on the outskirts of this forest."

"Oh, that's not a bad plan!"

"Glad to have helped," said Gaia, then she vanished in a swirl of mist.

The sun sank behind the mountains and cast huge shadows across the lake. Soon the shadows had all joined and the entire valley began the transition into night. Hector and Thomas shoved the canoe out onto the lake. They had waited till sunset hoping the limited light would help them avoid the eagle eyes of the drones. They hoped they could make it across the lake to Lana before nightfall.

The drones had flown back over the lake a couple of times whilst they had waited. However, the sky had been clear for the last hour so Hector and Thomas climbed aboard the canoe, Yorik and Grace hopped aboard after them. They paddled north along the edge of the lake, hugging the treeline as closely as they could in the failing light. Hector couldn't help looking back over his shoulder, scanning the sky for signs of movement. In the distance he could see the lights of Halmington, above them several lights seemed to be zipping back and forth across the sky, although he sincerely hoped that was his imagination.

The mood across the canoe was twitchy and nervous. With Hector in the rear regularly glancing back across the lake, and Thomas in the middle watching the bank for signs of movement. He was wondering if the search party had left a watch guard on the hill overnight. If they had, they would be seen as they crossed the small stretch of clear bank between the edge of the forest and the trees that lined the road to Lana. Thomas looked up at the clear sky above them, the moon would be up soon and they would be seen easily. Luckily however, clouds had started rolling in from the west.

The squirrels sat in the prow. Yorik was perched on the very point and was looking enigmatically out across the water. Grace laid with her back to him, dozing to the gentle sounds of water passing beneath her and rippling against the side of the boat.

"Why do you keep looking at the bank?" Hector asked Thomas.

"There's a bunch of people that I'd rather not run into."

"And they just happen to be wandering the cursed forest at this time of night?"

"Well . . ." Thomas turned and smiled at Hector. "They might have a few reasons for trying to find me."

"Because of your forced retirement?"

Thomas grimaced. He hated the word "retirement," it made him feel old. He also didn't believe what they were told about it either. The supposedly perfect town where you could finally rest and want for nothing. He could never accept that after a life of being lost in Lana, they would reward him with such a place.

"So, what are you going to do? Apart from helping me get Eve back," Thomas said blatantly refusing to answer the question.

"I don't know. Maybe after all this I'll go North into Suburbia. But I have a terrible feeling that I'll end up going West into . . . well, you know where."

"The Wastelands! You're not that desperate, are you?"

"It's the only place I can think of that they won't try and find me."

Thomas felt himself warming towards Hector, like they were kindred spirits thrown onto a difficult path together.

"They're trying to force me to go to Suburbia and I don't want to go there. Then these weird squirrels turned up."

"You do know we're not deaf, don't you?" said Yorik, breaking from his reverie.

"Or trying to sleep!" mumbled Grace, her eyes remaining closed.

"I'm still finding it hard to believe you actually exist, if it wasn't for Hector here—"

"And how do you know he actually exists?" asked Grace.

"Well, I guess I don't. But it's easier to believe he does exist than a talking squirrel!"

"There's no arguing with that kind of logical thinking," chided Grace.

Hector glared at Grace, wondering how far he could throw a squirrel across the lake.

"Pretty far I'd imagine, maybe even to the bank!" answered Thomas to the unasked question.

"What?" Yorik said. Hector cast a puzzled look at Thomas, had he really just answered the question in his head.

"Didn't you just ask how far you could throw a squirrel?" Thomas asked Hector.

"No! Well, not out loud, did I?" Hector said, now doubting his own actions.

"Ah, I see," said Grace. "Your power is starting to take effect."
"What?"
"You projected your thoughts into Thomas's head."
"I did what?"
"Your mind, it can project thoughts and feelings now."
"Oh. What do I–"
"Just embrace it as it comes." interrupted Grace.
"How do I control it then? Surely it will get irritating, me doing this to all of you!"
"That part is easy, when you feel your emotions starting to run away with you, imagine a solid wall of fire, encircling your being," answered Grace.
"Simple, you say?"
"We'll practice it when we reach Lana. I can show you what to do."

Half an hour of steady paddling and the trees on the bank started to thin. Suddenly there was nothing but the dark shadows of rolling hills in the distance, barely discernible from the skyline. They all scanned the horizon for any sign of the party chasing Thomas. Through the darkness they could make out little else but vague outlines. Then, from behind a ridge they saw the bright flickering of a small fire a little way up the dark outline of a hill. Luckily, it seemed as if they were too far away to be seen. Without the light of the moon they were thankfully hidden in the night.

They continued to paddle. All of their eyes were glued to the flickering distant light. In front of them the bank suddenly curved away from into a small bay. In the middle of the shoreline, a little way up from the water's edge, another fire roared. They stopped paddling and listened to the broken parts of conversation that floated over the water towards them. Grace got up and quietly joined Yorik.

Drifting slowly forwards they could make out the voices of several people. However, they couldn't make out the details of any of them. They would hear bits of several conversations all happening at once, then it would break into raucous laughter. Eventually their forward motion slowed without them paddling. They were nearly level with the fire. Yorik and Grace signaled for them to start paddling again, quietly. Thomas felt like each time he tried to slide the paddle into the water, the sloshing noise was deafening. Slowly they made their way across the bay. As they approached the edge of the campfire line of sight, suddenly they were bathed in silvery light. Thomas looked up at the bright full moon that had just burst through the clouds and betrayed them. They panicked and paddled for their lives, if they could just make it around the edge of the bay, they'd be safe. But it was too late, a cry called out from the bank and raised the alarm. They had been spotted. They threw everything they could into paddling and started to make good progress across the lake. However, as they started to tire, the resistance strangely decreased. It seemed as if there was a current carrying them towards the middle of the lake. A gentle breeze wafted them that way too. Gaia, Thomas thought, even unseen, she still helped them through the currents of the waters and air. They would risk losing their way in the middle of the lake but it beat being shot at or grabbed from the shoreline. The water swished below them as they sped along, the bank grew further away. Thomas looked back towards the bay where the shoreline was now dancing with the light from small handheld torches. The lights were beginning to move along the bank, keeping up with their progress down the lake.

Gaia once more intervened and the silvery light that bathed them vanished. The moon returned to its resting place behind the thick storm clouds above them. After the moment of elation passed, they panicked. They were floating somewhere in the middle of the lake with only the light from the mercenaries chasing them. They had no idea which direction they were heading. But then, fortune smiled on them. In the far distance, they could just make out the twinkling lights of Lana, or at least what they hoped was Lana. After what seemed like an age of paddling, the small harbour of Lana drew closer. All along the small curved bay, wooden structures that resembled houses backed out onto the water. A few had their own private jetties.

"So where are we landing?" asked Thomas.

"They're going to be on us in less than an hour wherever we dock," said Hector.

"Do you still own your house by the water Thomas?" asked Yorik.

"Yeah, but if you're thinking we should head there, surely that'll be the first place they look?"

"They will, but I have a plan. Take us there."

"Plan? What is it?"

"I'll tell you when we get inside."

If there had been the light to see each other's faces by, then Yorik would have seen the confused and very suspicious look Thomas was giving him.

"Which one is it?" asked Hector.

"That one over there," said Thomas pointing to the right. "The one next to the one with the red lantern outside it."

"Red lantern?" asked Hector.

"Yeah, that's our neighbour, Miss Feelgood and Mr. Happy. Well, I'm not sure if that's their real names, but it's what the locals call them."

"Oh, I see," said Hector, finally catching up.

A light seemed to go on in Yoriks head too.

"So you live next to a—"

"They moved in after we did! I have you know that Lakeside is some of the best housing in Lana!" Thomas spat back.

"Not saying much, though, is it, really?" chided Grace.

Thomas growled and plunged his paddle into the water, turning the boat to the right quite violently. They started paddling once again, this time in the general direction of Thomas's house, or the red light of the distant brothel.

Lana

They reached the small jetty and tied up the canoe. Thomas looked out across the bay as they stood on the Jetty. Torch lights were still moving quickly along the edge of the lake and heading towards them.
Inside the house, Thomas led them to his modest kitchen. Unsurprisingly things were exactly as he had left them yesterday morning.
"Sorry about the mess, I had to leave in a bit of a hurry," said Thomas.
"It's fine, you should see my place," replied Hector. He thought back to his own immaculate home. With his wife in the hospital he often found himself compulsively cleaning when he was alone. Telling Thomas about that obviously wouldn't help though.
"So, what's the plan?" Thomas asked Yorik.
"It's quite simple really, when they come to search the place, all you need to do is think of Carla."
"Think of Carla? What kind of stupid plan is that?" asked Hector.
"Actually, that might work," said Thomas.
"Oh! The transforming thing! That can work for humans too?"
"It should work for anyone or anything," said Yorik.
Not for the first time, Hector had a strange feeling in his gut. The Carla that Thomas talked of, surely couldn't be the Carla he used to know? The same person that had cursed his wife? But then again,

weirder coincidences have happened. He decided to put it to the back of his mind; he would find out soon enough.

Thomas guided them into a large sitting room. They settled down into the comfortable armchairs and a sofa that were centered around a large stone fireplace. Thomas offered everyone drinks whilst Hector lit a fire. Soon they were warm, comfortable and despite the impending danger, beginning to doze.

After about half an hour they were jolted awake by a commotion outside. Thomas peeked through the windows. Further up the dark street Thomas could see a large band of people making their way down towards them. The crowd was banging on each of the doors with their torches and barging into them to conduct violating searches.

"You need to start thinking about Carla, right now!" said Yorik.

"What? I'm freaking out! How am I supposed to think about her?"

"Look around you, this is the place you shared, the place you brought Eve into the world. Remember your wife, the good times you shared here."

Thomas gazed off hazily into the distance, his mind lost in memories. There was an unsettling squelching noise as his face and body slowly morphed into the shape of Carla.

Hector stared into the face of the woman he had been harbouring such hate for all these years. The reason his wife was probably nothing more than ashes right now. How come such a monster had taken over the loving Carla he once knew? He felt the rage boil inside him. Hector clenched his fists and felt his face flush. He wanted to scream at her face. He needed to vent his anger towards her and make her feel the pain he did. Thomas would understand and agree, he would probably even sympathise with him. But a thought tapped at the edges of his anger. This wasn't really Carla. The thought trickled through his tortured mind and slowly doused his enraged feelings.

He regained control and realised that such a conversation would also lead to questions. Questions about when and where he had met Carla. At that moment an incredibly obvious thought struck him. Thomas was the man Carla was married to when he had an affair with her! His mind reeled, he needed time to get his head round this. He clamped his mouth shut and stared at the floor.

"That's brilliant Thomas! Just keep that up," encouraged Yorik, oblivious to Hector's internal torment.

"Hmm," Thomas said.

"Just remember, leave the talking to me. Just be haughty and aloof, keep thinking about Carla."

"Grace, grab Hector."

"Eh? But what the hell?"

"Oh, come on Hector, you know they'll have heard about you, they'll be looking for you everywhere."
"Are you okay Hector?" asked Grace, feeling the turbulence inside Hector.
"We're about to get interrogated by soldiers and mercenaries, I'm anxious! Won't they be a little suspicious seeing two giant squirrels?" he asked, desperate to change the subject.
"We have that covered." Yorik motioned to Hector's side, where Grace had just scampered to.
"No offense, but I don't think they'll believe I'm being held by a squirrel—" Hector turned to look at Grace, but instead of the large squirrel, there was a rough looking man in his place. The man was wearing the scruffy but effective leathers of the local law enforcement. As Hector looked incredulously at what he presumed was Grace, the man meekly waved back at him.
Hector turned back to Yorik but he had also been replaced by a female version of the scruffy looking man, another agent of the local law enforcement.
"This shape shifting stuff is bloody unnerving," Hector grumbled.
There was a loud bang on the door, followed by several more.
"Open up!" a voice yelled from the outside.
Yorik snapped into character. He unbolted the front door and swung it open.

"Who dares interrupt The Councillor?" Yorik proclaimed.

"We — What? The Councillor? What are you on about?" said the disheveled mercenary. Either side of him stood two equally untidy looking characters.

"The Councillor, Carla, has temporarily resumed habitation of her old house, whilst she personally apprehends the escaped debtor Hector Winterslow."

"Hector Winterslow? You mean that runner from south of the lake? The one that got all them drones buzzing? Why would she care about a debtor?"

"Carla has a personal interest in him."

"Really? Who are you then? I don't recognise you at all. What unit are you from?"

"Not that it's any of your business, but we are with Epsilon Psi."

"Epsilon Psi? I never even heard of that unit!"

"We're the secret security force to the Head Councillor. Of course you haven't heard of us, no one has." answered Yorik.

"I know every unit. I have access at the highest level. I'm in charge of the unit that will be escorting The Councillor and her daughter to the Caverns."

"What!" cried Thomas's rough voice from the living room.

"Who's that?" the guard asked.

"That is . . . erm, The Counselor. She has a bad case of laryngitis."

"Laren-what?"

"She can't talk." added Grace helpfully.
The mercenaries seemed suspicious, one of them went to reach for a shiny pistol shaped object hung by his waist.
"Fine, don't believe us, wait here." Yorik slammed the door in their faces and walked back into the living room.
"Eve really is alive!" cried Thomas.
"Shhh, You're voice!" said Yorik. "We're going to have to let him in. Follow my lead, and don't talk!"
"The Councillor?" asked Thomas.
"It's a long story, I'll tell you later. Just act haughtily, like you own the world."
"How am I supposed to do that without speaking?"
"I don't know, just act!"
Yorik walked back over to the door and snatched it open.
"The Councillor will see you now, but I warn you, she has lost her voice and is quick to anger."
The foremost mercenary looked taken aback, he had expected a feeble reason that he couldn't see her.
"Right, well,"
"This way." Yorik gestured to the living room.
The mercenary nodded to the people by his side and strode into the room by himself. He stopped in his tracks as his eyes met the cold stare of The Councillor, or so he thought.
Even though Thomas was sitting whilst everyone around him stood, he managed to seem like he was

looking down on the occupants of the room. Yorik was impressed with his silent acting.

"Ma'am, forgive my intrusion but I had to be sure Thomas wasn't here. I haven't had the pleasure of meeting these guards before."

Thomas's cold steely eyes stared straight through the soldier. Thomas, now fully in character of his ex, was longing to scold him and tell him to bugger off. But he kept quiet."

"As you can see, he isn't here and The Councillor is very busy—"

"Oh absolutely, my apologies, surprised to find you here. We were diverted to pick up Thomas, on our way to Burnim for an escort mission for you and the Lady Eve-"

"Eve!" cried Thomas, his deep voice booming from the slender figure of Carla. The mercenary looked startled and confused.

"As I said, The Councillor has laryngitis, she doesn't sound herself at the moment," said Yorik. "She was referring to how you knew the movement plans of The Councillor?"

"Well it's the detail of the job?"

"Detail?"

"On the outsourcing form we get for each contract."

"Oh, the security team really have those efficiencies nailed down don't they?" sighed Grace.

"What?" said the soldier.

"Plans have changed somewhat since Thomas went on the run. What was on your latest contract?" asked Grace.

The mercenary eyed her suspiciously.

"We were supposed to report to the Tower by the end of the week. With or without Thomas."

"For an escort contract?"

"Yes, but doesn't The Councillor already know this? She was the one who gave the order—"

"Watch your attitude! A lot has changed in the Capital and she wishes to know how much you have been privy to."

"I received the order two days ago."

"Who from? And what did it say?"

"Like I said already, we are to report to Burnim by the end of the week to escort The Councillor and her daughter to the Caverns. It was from the Security and People Management team in Burnim tower."

The words echoed through Thomas's mind, he couldn't believe it, his daughter really was alive! Yorik winced, feeling Thomas's volatile state.

"Councillor, may I suggest we cancel that order, we can monitor the Tower and see who reacted to it. That will point to our mole. If I may?" he said looking directly at Thomas.

Thomas stared right through him, his mind raced with confused emotions and the wild imagings of his thoughts. He blinked and returned to reality. He nodded at Yorik in approval.

"Continue looking for Thomas South of the lake. Do not report to the Tower, nor speak of seeing the Councillor today. If anyone asks; you have received another order to go South via the forest, understood?"
The mercenary looked confused and a little worried.
"The forest? Do we really have to?"
"You don't have to travel through the forest. Take the road through the mountains and circle back on the other side. The longer you are on the road away from communications the better."
"Oh, but—"
"There are more things going on at the Tower than you could possibly imagine. Trust in The Councillor and stay loyal to her. You will be rewarded when this is over."
"That's great to hear, but we don't work on credit as I'm sure you're aware."
"You haven't completed the other contract yet?"
"But only because you changed the details, it's not the same now."
"How about we double the rate, you keep the half upfront you had from the other contract?"
The mercenary pondered on the offer.
"Double the rate!"
"Fine, double." agreed Thomas.
The tension in the room dissolved and the mercenary looked very happy.

"Keep out of the way and do not speak of anything that has just been said, especially about the mole." said Grace.

"I will, confidentiality is our company core values." The mercenary quickly left.

Yorik closed the door behind him and turned back to Thomas. He was morphing back into his real body.

"My daughter is still alive!" he cried..

"Shhhh, he might be hanging around outside," whispered Grace. "I don't think he was entirely convinced by our ruse. It was only the fear of Carla that made him go."

"But . . . she's alive," Thomas whispered back.

"We thought she might have been. In fact, we pinned our hopes on it. We need to get to Burnim," said Yorik.

"So, how do we do that then?" asked Hector.

"We wait until the morning and head North to the Suburbs."

"Disguised?" asked Thomas.

"Yeah. Possibly all the way. There will be a lot of guards ferrying people up there I imagine," said Yorik.

"I'm not sure I can keep it up for that long! It was hard enough to just sit here and I didn't even have to say anything."

"You'll be fine. Now we better get some sleep. We may not have much chance for any rest after tonight."

They all agreed and sunk into the comfortable seats around the fire. Thomas fetched some blankets and handed them around.

"You said you'd teach me how to control my mind," said Hector.

Grace turned to Hector, weariness tugging at her eyelids.

"Ok Hector, you're right, I did. But it will have to be a short session I'm afraid. Close your eyes."

Hector closed his eyes, instantly he could hear Grace talking to him. However, it wasn't regular speech, it was as if the voice was coming from inside his head, a point between his eyes.

Can you hear me, Hector?

"Yes! I can hear you!" Hector cried out loud. It startled Thomas and he jumped out of his descent into sleep.

"What the hell?" Thomas asked.

He can't hear us, rather than talking, imagine you are saying what you want to.

Hector looked at Grace, and sure enough her mouth never moved.

"Sorry Thomas, I was answering Grace."

Thomas looked at Hector, shook his head and snuggled deeper into the chair.

You mean like this? Hector asked in his head.

That's it. Now, think of your mind as a delicate squidgy ball. If you don't control what comes in and out of it, you can damage it, or others. The easiest way to control this is to imagine a column of white light, springing from deep below the Earth, to the skies above. Then imagine another light, a clear light, coming down from the skies above and passing deep into the Earth. At the center you are protected. It is like your own cocoon of protection.

Ok. Hector imagined a beautiful column of pure white light, it made him feel very peaceful. Then he layered the clear light over the top and he felt protected from all directions. He felt completely safe and protected.
Good, that's good, I can feel the resistance.
So how can I still hear you?
I've been doing this a long time Hector; I can pierce your mental barriers quite easily and hear only what I need to. One day you may become strong enough to resist anyone.
Can anyone with this power break through the wall?
Only if they are skilled at it. Relax, you are still safe.
I won't be able to keep everyone out?
The mind is like a muscle, if you exercise it, it will grow stronger. However, it is unlikely you are the strongest out there, so there will always be some who can break your barriers. But, very good Hector, I can feel your barrier gaining strength. Now, keep practicing that. Tomorrow I'll show you how to create one that you can control what gets in and out of it.

Grace and Hector opened their eyes, Yorik had curled up by the fire and Thomas was gazing sleepily out the window. Grace hopped over to join Yorik by the fire.
"I thought you were tired, Tom?" asked Hector.
"I was, but then some noisy bugger woke me up and I can't get the thought of Eve out of my head now."
"Sorry."
Thomas and Hector chatted quietly about Eve until the night turned into early morning and they fell asleep.

A Small World

A few hours later, after a hurried breakfast, Thomas disguised himself once more as Carla and they walked out through the front door into a bright sunny morning.

They headed towards the town center and turned right to head up the high street. It cut straight through the heart of the town and then turned to head North. The street was almost empty. The houses that leaned on each other for support hid the nocturnal folk that slumbered within. Only a handful of respectable people were going about their daily business, proud in the delusion they were pretty much the only respectable people in Lana. Everyone who came within view of Thomas, still disguised as Carla, crossed the road to avoid them. Most kept their heads down and pretended not to have seen them.

By late morning they were beginning to reach the outskirts of the town and started to climb the dusty road that led out of the valley.

The houses were further apart and they seemed more like farms than townhouses. These could actually stand by themselves and looked rather well built. They passed a rough looking pub with a wooden sign swinging on the post outside. On the sign was the painted picture of a cartoon duck being stretched over a rack. Underneath the picture were the words

'Tortured Duck'. Outside the door there was a blackboard sign, on it was chalked the words
'Qiz Nite Tonite!'
Leaning against the wall around the front door there were a couple of disheveled looking people, all of them smoking some form of pipe. As they passed the doorway the tallest of the group called out.
"Hey there! How's things Thomas?" he said with a friendly countryside accent.
Thomas looked down at himself, he was still disguised as Carla.
"What?" he tried to ask pompously, but failed.
"Who dares address The Councillor in such a manner?" said Yorik.
As the man approached, Thomas looked into his eyes and recognised a face he had not seen for years.
"Wilf?" asked Thomas.
"Long time no see eh, Thomas!"
"Yorik, Grace, this is Wilf, he's Carla's father."
"Oh," said Yorik.
"How did you know it was me?" Thomas asked.
"Well, you don't think I can't see through that child's magic?"
"What! Do you know about this? You never mentioned—"
"There's somethings you just don't talk about around ere." Wilf said, looking back over his shoulder to the people leaning against the pub. They were craning

their necks and cupping their ears in a vain attempt to eavesdrop on their conversation.

They walked further away from them and the crowd by the pub lost hope of catching any news and returned to their conversations.

"How can you see me then?"

"It's complicated, anyway, so where's you off to then?"

"Erm, the Suburbs. We're escorting Hector there," answered Yorik.

"Oh yeah, that's right," he replied, eyeing them suspiciously. He gave a friendly nod towards Hector.

"Have you seen Carla recently?" Thomas asked.

"A while back, you should try talking to her, Tom. She's not as angry as she used to be. It broke my heart when I heard you two split."

"Did you know about Eve?" Thomas barked, unable to contain his anger.

Wilf held Thomas's stare, then swallowed hard and looked down at the floor.

"Yeah, I did. Sorry. She made me keep it a deep secret. I was really sorry you had to go through all that. That wasn't right, I tried to stop her but—"

"How the hell could you let that happen!" he cried.

The people at the pub door stood up straight and stared at them again.

"Carla's my little girl, Tom. Wouldn't you have done the same to protect Eve?"

"But she made me think she was dead!"

"I know, I know, like I said, that wasn't right, I'm sorry."
Thomas could see the sorrow in Wilf's eyes. Despite the rage boiling inside him he felt a deep connection to him. He had been caught between his and Carla's insanity.
"Look Wilf. I get it, it's not your fault. I only found out yesterday."
"Of course, it must be all a bit raw. So, who's your friends here?" Wilf asked.
"They're Yorik and Grace, I'm Hector." Hector answered.
"They're interesting things, aren't they."
"We're right here you know!" exclaimed Grace.
"You mean you see them as the giant squirrel things?" asked Hector.
"Squirrels? Hmm interesting."
"Why is it interesting?"
"Oh, no reason really."
"Don't you see the squirrels?"
Yorik and Grace looked at each other and shifted uneasily.
"It doesn't matter. Look, why don't you stop for a drink? We can continue this inside."
"Thanks, but I'm afraid we can't. We have a long way to go today. We hope to make it to the Suburbs by tonight."
"Suburbs eh? That's some trek. Why are you going there anyway?"

"It's his time." said Yorik pointing to Hector.

"His time? It was yours too from what I heard." Wilf said, pointing at Thomas. "Why would you do that then? I heard you were on the run? I was so glad; thought you had seen sense."

"Why? What's wrong with the Suburbs?" asked Hector.

"You'll see. But do yourselves a favour, leave the road a mile or two before the gates and approach it through the trees. You'll be glad you do."

"Ah, ok, thanks."

"Wilf, I'm sorry to seem rude, but how come they haven't come to collect you?" asked Thomas.

Wilf smirked. "You aint the only one who can perform magic, Tom."

"Really?"

"I'll explain it all if you stop for a drink."

"Thanks, but we really must go."

"Will you tell Carla about seeing us?" blurted Hector.

Wilf looked at him and smiled fondly.

"Hector, I ain't forgotten our friendship, y'know. All I can promise is that I won't deliberately tell her."

"You know each other?" asked Thomas.

"We- er- used to enter quizzes together. In this very pub if I remember." At least part of that was true, Hector thought.

"That's right, a while back now. Used to have a right laugh at ol Hector here, he was great at the science round, but didn't know his arse from a hole in the ground when it came to general knowledge!"

"'Deliberately tell her'? What does that mean?" asked Thomas.

"It means if she asks me directly, I'll tell her. I can't lie to my own daughter, not for anyone."

"So you won't tell her then?"

"No, but it's only fair to warn you, she sent for me an hour ago, was just finishing my drink and I'll be off."

"You know where she is?"

"Sure, that's no secret. She's in her ivory tower in Burnim."

"Ivory tower?" asked Thomas.

"It's not really ivory, it's just a tower." Wilf clarified.

"Well, thanks Wilf, we really must be off now though." Yorik urged.

Wilf shook their hands and walked back to the pub. He rejoined his friends as they returned to leaning against the wall.

Eve

On the one hundred and ninetieth floor of the tallest building in the city of Burnim, a girl sat cross-legged on the edge of a luxuriously soft rug. The room was sparsely decorated but in a deliberate way that ensured it was at the very edge of cutting fashion. The girl was about thirteen years old, she had cascading auburn hair and piercing blue eyes. Her natural unpolished beauty seemed out of place in the sleek modern and superficial world around her.

In front of her was a long low coffee table made almost completely of glass. Hovering above it a ball of fire danced within the confines of an invisible sphere. She was in control of that sphere. It was the projection of an energy barrier created by harnessing the power of her being. She stretched it into a long cylinder and smiled as the flames inside cajoled into the new shape. The dance of fire intrigued her in the same way it had entranced generations of humans before her.

Even with the calm state of mind she had to be in to create the wonderful spectacle in front of her, she was fighting feelings of frustration. Technically she wasn't a prisoner in the tower. But she was rarely allowed to leave the tower and her mother insisted she always have a guard with her when she did.

She extinguished the fire and dissolved the bubble, letting the remaining ash to fall onto the table. A small hovering sanitation robot appeared from behind her. It sank to the table and cleaned the ashes up. When it had finished and flew back out of the room, the table was spotless.

In an attempt to alleviate her boredom, she stretched out the tendrils of her being and sensed all the people in the tower. She felt the people as small fields of light and could recognise most of them by subtle differences or 'feelings' about them. Some were different colours, some burnt brightly, some were dim and others flickered from dark to light.

She sought out the scientists and lab technicians on the lower levels. These were the most interesting she had found. Eve slowly felt her way through each light shape. The majority were busy with their experiments or paperwork, but then she found one of the lead scientists, Chad. She had probed Chad's mind before and it had always proved interesting and enlightening. She joined a tendril from her mind to his subconscious and started to see through his eyes. He was staring at a large glass panel filled with numbers and touch sensitive areas. She probed deeper to try and decipher them. He was performing experiments on someone to enhance their mental abilities.

This would have been shocking but it wasn't the first time she had found him doing this. His latest attempts had shown promising results though. However, the people he regarded as subjects had always rejected the enhancements after a week or two and ended up technically brain dead.

"Eve!" a voice called to her through her mental wanderings. It came from the room where her body was sitting.

"Eve," the voice called again, it sounded like her mother.

Eve disentangled herself from Chad's mind and slowly returned to her body. The process had to be done carefully or it could cause all manner of problems, for her and Chad.

"Mother?" she said, opening her eyes. Carla stood across the table from her. Her long black hair was flecked with grey strands of age. Her emerald green eyes stared down at her.

"We need to talk."

Carla led Eve to her large private study and she sat down behind the solid wooden desk that dominated the room. She gestured for Eve to take the leather seat opposite. She leaned forward on the desk and touched her finger tips together. Something seemed to be bothering her, thought Eve.

"Eve, I have something to tell you. I imagine you might already suspect."

"What's wrong, Mother?"

She frowned. "Why don't you ever call me Mum? Mother sounds so—"

"Cold?" ventured Eve.

Her mother eyed her cautiously. "I was going to say formal. Do you think I'm cold?"

"Well, you dragged me here, you refuse to talk to me about dad. I think that's cold!"
"Don't start that again, I brought us here to protect us. As for your father, there is nothing more to tell you about him."
"Why do you never let me see him?"
"He died! I sent a team to trace him but they found nothing. Why do you keep asking these same questions? My answers never change, they're the truth!"
"I don't believe you."
Carla held Eve's glaring stare, then sighed. "I wish you'd believe me. But even if you don't, come your eighteenth birthday you are more than welcome to go looking for him yourself. When you find his gravestone, you can send him my regards."
"And you ask if you're cold!"
"Look, this isn't what I wanted to talk about. I may be cold, as you say, but it's only because sometimes in life you have to do unpleasant things, things that seem wrong but are actually vital in making things better."
"What are you talking about?"
"Eve, I know you know probe the minds of the scientists in the tower. We've been monitoring your activity in Chad's mind."
"Oh."
"It's okay, I'm not angry. I'm impressed if anything, but I just want you to understand about the experiments."

"Understand?"

"It's not just my company being cruel to people and carelessly making them brain dead. There's a reason why it's happening and although it's unpleasant for the people, they are actually helping the survival of our species."

"Survival of our species?"

"It's complicated, but simply put, they are helping us create humans to face the next challenges the universe throws at us."

"What challenges?"

"Again, it's complicated. There are things out there in the universe that want to take our planet from us, or even worse."

"What?"

"You'll have so many questions I imagine. So I want you to see it for yourself, I want you to visit the lab. Then you can find out exactly what we are doing and why."

"Really? I can go down there?"

"Yes, Dr. Wilson is on his way up to collect you as we speak."

At that moment, almost on cue, there was a pleasant chiming sound from the door.

"Yes."

A tall, slender woman with hair pulled into a tight bun appeared at the doorway.

"Ma'am, Dr. Wilson is here to see you."

"Great, show him in."

She stood and beckoned Eve to follow her to the door. They met the doctor as he entered the room.

"Doctor, exactly on time. Could you show Eve the labs as we discussed earlier? Give her as much time as she wants. Answer any questions she has."

"Yes Ma'am."

The doctor and Eve left the room. He led her down corridors and towards the elevators. Her mother waited until they were both out of earshot then turned to the lady with the tight bun.

"Jane, once Eve is inside the lab shielding, let my father through the front entrance and bring him to my office."

"Yes Ma'am."

The Tower of Hidden Chambers

The doctor and Eve rode the elevator down to the seventh floor. Whilst they stood in uncomfortable silence as the digital display counted down the floor numbers, she gently probed the doctor's mind. It was strange, in all her mental wanderings she'd never encountered his mind shape before.

The elevator pinged and the doors slid open. The gleaming white corridors of the laboratory floor dazzled her eyes as they stepped from the elevator.

"This is the research center, Eve. We have more than thirty laboratories in all."

"What do they do?"

"A number of fascinating things," he said enthusiastically.

"Like what?" Eve asked, desperate to ask about the room she could never see into from upstairs.

"Well, in one we're trying to help people develop certain abilities."

"Like how to fly?" she asked, deliberately goading the doctor.

He eyed Eve nervously. "Well sort of, we tried that a while back but had no success. We are focusing more on the ways we can develop our minds to do things that would help us all."

"You mean like reading minds?"

The doctor shifted his weight and started to squirm uneasily. He had obviously heard of her powers. Eve half suspected he had 'experimented' on her in the past. There were several dark patches in his mind she couldn't penetrate.

"Yes, we are experimenting a lot with that. But telepathy is more than mind reading, Eve. Telepathy means you can 'talk' to people with that similar ability. Imagine how wonderful it would be if we stopped misunderstanding each other because of our poor use of languages. People would know what you really mean to say because they could read your thoughts at the purest level."

A tall man in a white lab coat appeared from one of the side doors. He looked as if he hadn't seen sunlight for quite some time.

"Ah, Dr. Wilson, we have just finished–"

"James, let me introduce you to Eve."

James seemed shocked, as if he had just seen a monster. He quickly recovered and composed himself.

"A pleasure, Eve." Said James.

"What do you mean 'misunderstanding'?" Eve asked the doctor, keeping her eyes on James.

"Well, have you ever had a time when you tried to tell someone something, but the words didn't come out right or the other person didn't understand what you were trying to say?"

"Yeah, sometimes."

"If we could figure out how to make everyone have telepathic abilities, we might all understand each other more easily and we could bring peace to this planet!"

"Ever the optimist! You see Eve, Dr. Wilson here thinks flicking a switch in our brains will make everyone suddenly be nice to each other." Said James.

"And why is that so hard to believe?" asked Dr. Wilson.

"Well, just because we can read each other's minds, it doesn't stop bad people from having bad thoughts," replied James.

"I disagree, I think it would. Why do you think most people have bad thoughts and misguided intentions?" asked Dr. Wilson.

"For many reasons, I guess. Bad upbringing, people being nasty to them, a whole host of psychological issues possibly."

"If you examine all of the reasons, barring the physical and psychological, they could be traced back to some misunderstanding. Or maybe they have been hurt by people who acted without empathy. Usually it's the narcissists that ironically need the most love, but not in the way they think they need it. Either way telepathy would let us understand what our fellow humans have been through and how they feel and think." Said the doctor.

"But isn't that dangerous?" asked Eve.

The doctor looked at Eve quizzically. "What do you mean?"

"It seems to me that lots of people might have thoughts that they don't want others to know, thoughts they keep hidden because they're worried about what people might think of them if they knew they were having them." Said Eve.

The doctor looked at Eve with a frightened reverence, she seemed too young to be having such insights and thoughts. He knew from his experiments on her when she was younger that she would be powerful, but she really was growing into something special. It made him slightly uncomfortable.

"You're right, Eve, people do have thoughts and feelings like that. But the thing is, once we unlock telepathy, people will change. We won't have those dark corners in our heads, we will be open to the world. It's a scary thought but people will adapt. Once we all realise that half the thoughts we have, we share with everyone, we'll feel connected again."

"But what about the other thoughts? The really bad ones that run through our minds that we might not actually want to be thinking about?" asked Eve.

"Those will be difficult to manage but I think it will be fine. People will realise that their hidden private thoughts aren't anything to hide, they're actually similar to many other people's, or that other people's hidden thoughts are no worse or better than their own. It might actually be a good side effect, people will lose their feelings of guilt and realise thoughts like that are what they actually are, nothing." The doctor said.

"Do you really think people wouldn't react to finding out someone harboured bad thoughts or intentions about them?" asked James.

"You miss one of the most powerful parts of telepathy, that is you gain empathy. You wouldn't hate those people any more than they hate you. You would feel what they felt, and they would feel what you did. With understanding would come compassion." The doctor replied.

"You mean we might realise that we're all a bit weird?" asked Eve.

The doctor laughed.

"Yes, I guess we would. But look at it this way, we'll stop thinking of ourselves as weird and realise we're all actually quite normal in our uniqueness. We'll feel part of the world rather than outsiders trying to fit in."

"That does sound nice."

The doctor looked at an illuminated patch of skin on his wrist and it visibly agitated him.

"Right Eve, we must be moving on. If you could follow me into this lab, you'll see some of the experiments we do here."

The doctor ushered Eve through the nearest doorway. As Eve crossed the threshold, she felt something change. Like walking into an air-conditioned room when it's baking hot outside. Something was dramatically different in this room. Then she understood where she was. It was where the mind shape's she usually felt in the building had vanished into. She figured they must have gone inside this room. The room was dark, lit only by a bank of computer screens that lined the wall on the right. In front of them stood several men and women in white lab coats. They were examining the monitors and making notes. On the other wall to their left, a glass partition separated the room from a ward of six beds. Eve could see that in each clinically white bed there was a person they were experimenting on.

"So, Eve, this is our more intense experimentation lab. We have a couple like this that I'll show you later, but this is the main one. You may have felt the extra shielding we had to put over it when we entered. As you can see our scientists carefully monitor the subjects and over here, we can see the latest round of experiments."

"Why the extra shielding?"

"Some of the experiments can have some rather powerful effects on the subjects. The extra shielding stops anything from getting out, or damaging the building."

"What have you done to them?"

"They have been given a solution to promote genetic mutation. It's supposed to enhance psychokinetic abilities."

"Psycho— what?"

"The ability to move things with your mind."

"Oh, like making things float and stuff."

"Yes, that's it."

"So, can they make stuff move now?"

"No, not yet. We're trying to help them develop the ability. You see, the formula we gave them helps their bodies develop the ability, but that doesn't mean they know how to do it. It's like we have helped them grow wings and now they just need to learn how to fly."

"Does it take long for them to learn?"

"We don't know, Eve. They've had the ability for a week now, but they don't seem to be getting anywhere."

"Have you tried helping them?"

"We've been giving them tests every hour and we have left several soft objects in there for them to experiment with. But to be honest, we're not sure how to 'help' them. It's something we can't do ourselves; we have no idea how."

"You mean none of you know how it works?"

"Well, no. We don't have the ability."

The doctor looked nervously at Eve. Although he had experimented on her in the past, he feared what letting her loose in a room full of experimental subjects would do. Would she be able to control her powers?

"Yeah, I can make things float and stuff." Eve answered the unspoken question.

The whole room dropped into silence and all attention fell on Eve.

"You mean you can move things with just your mind?" said one of the lab assistants.

"Yeah," she answered simply.

"W— we— well how long have you been able to do it?"

"I can't really remember when I first did it. But I do remember practicing loads. I spent a whole summer trying to make things fly, then eventually I could."
"Do you remember how you learned to do that?"
"Yeah, kinda, I think."
"Do you think you could teach them?" the doctor said, pointing at the people in the beds beyond the glass screen.
"I guess I could try showing them what I know?"
"Could you do that, Eve? Would you? It would really help our results but I'll need to check with Car— your mother. It could be very dangerous since you might need to go in there."
"Go in there?" she asked, pointing to the room.
"Yeah, if you need to use your mind you won't be able to get past the shielding."
"I can't get past the shielding?"
"Yeah, it's specially designed to deaden and stop mental energies from entering or escaping that room."
"You think you really need it?"
"We need to be safe here. Imagine what would happen if one of them started making things fly around the office! Or even worse, take control of our minds."
"Oh, I see. But it's alright, I can get past it, I think. It's not that strong. I just need to find a point I can break through."
"Eve, be careful, wait until we—"
Eve didn't wait and was already diving into the depths of her mind; the doctor's words were lost on her. She

reached out the tendrils of her consciousness and could see the translucent boundary of shielding surrounding the ward of people. She pushed gently at the edge and it wobbled like a giant bubble. She pushed harder and felt herself slip through it. The bubble sealed neatly behind her.

She projected her conscious thoughts into the room and her mind exploded. All around her the patients on the beds were mentally screaming out in agony. She felt their pain, anger, frustration, and hatred all rolled into vicious purple balls of raw emotion. The balls of emotion grew around the people's heads until they looked like they were about to explode. Just before they did, they snapped the tether to the patients and started to bounce around the inside of the bubble shield. One of them passed right through her and she felt every part of it. From the terror they had experienced being captured by armed guards to the hatred they felt for the scientists as they were strapped down, injected, and studied. The torrent of concentrated emotions was unbearable. She raced to escape the bubble shield but it would not let her back out. Every point she tried to push through gave and bent to compensate for her pressure and would not let her through. Another sphere of emotion passed through her. She screamed. All around her she saw the spheres and there was no way she could stop them. She focused all her might on pushing through the bubble. Finally, when she was about to give up, the bubble wall stopped moving. It felt like a taught elastic band stretched to breaking point. She pushed a little more and the bubble popped.

In the physical world the bursting of the shielding caused a cacophony of alarms to ring out across the laboratory floor. The purple emotion spheres were now freed and they careened through the mental plane, ripping through any mind they came into contact with. Two of the lab assistants were screaming, and one of the doctors fell to the floor in tears.

The laboratory doors burst open as everyone piled out of the room. They sprinted straight towards the elevators. White-coated scientists spilled out from all the other labs into the corridor, looking around in confusion. The alarms were deafening. Everyone seemed to have forgotten about Eve in the panic. She slipped away from the stampede and headed the opposite way up the corridor. At the first junction she turned down a corridor on her left. She followed it to a plain sliding door marked 'Service Elevator'. Eve pressed the button and waited for the lift to clunk its way down to her. The doors parted noisily revealing a metal cage that was open to the lift workings above and below. She got in and typed ninety-eight into the grubby keypad. A dated display panel lit up with the floor number she was on and the one she had just typed in. As the lift doors shut the cage shuddered upwards, accelerating slowly into the dark shaft above.

Fatherly Advice

As she rose a few floors, the alarms were quietened. Presumably, they had managed to restore the force fields and reset the alarms.

Eve felt around for the energy shapes of all the people in the building. She sought the familiar shape of her mother, wondering how angry she was going to be. Carla was up on the very top floor, in her office, her mind seemed quite calm. She couldn't actually see colours, but she felt them. It always seemed to her that calm minds were a cool blue, and angry was a violent red. There was a whole range of colours in-between that could help you understand the being. Eve was still trying to figure out all their meanings, there were so many. Carla's mind was mainly blue with a tinge of red at the edges, something must be annoying her. She wondered if it was the news about the chaos she had just caused. But it didn't feel like it. She imagined her mother would be a lot angrier about that. Eve noticed that there was another prominent energy shape very close to her, it felt like it was in the same room. It wasn't a shape she had seen in the building before but it did look familiar for some reason.

She looked at the lift display, the floor number had just flickered to fifteen. Having nothing better to do she probed the unknown entity a little further. She had an eerie sense of familiarity. It was as if she had known the shape intimately in the past, but it was more than that. This shape was a lot like her own. It wasn't exactly the same, but there was a lot they had in common.

She sent the tendrils of her being into the open parts of the energy shape. It was male, seemingly a kindly person. He had just traveled from Lana. Something had upset the man, he had actually been summoned! Carla had called him to the tower. Quite urgently it seems because the man was quite agitated.

Eve reached the border between his conscious and subconscious mind when she felt something. His subconscious was protected. She was pretty sure he wasn't aware of her yet, but if she crossed the border he would instantly know she was there. There was a strange sense of power from him.

Eve tried to listen to the conversation they were having. This was a trick she had only recently learned. It involved focusing intently on the mental effects the exchange between them was having. Eve imagined it to be like turning up the sensitivity on a microphone so she could hear the distant echoes of a conversation.

It was her mother she heard first.

"Dad, stop pissing about, just tell me what you know!"
"Well, we'd be here a while if I told you all that I know! Fair few years of knowledge in this cabbage you know. Admit some of it's a little hazy, some a little crazy, as I've been stewin it in alcohol for the last—"
"DAD! What the hell did Thomas say to you?"
"How d'you know I spoke with Thomas?"

"I have my ways of finding things out."
"Spies?"
"I prefer the term 'Guardians of Council Interest'"
"Oh right, spies then. Is Billy one?"
"Billy? No dad, you don't know them."
"I always imagined Billy to be a spy, either that or a pirate. Anyone with an eye patch like his looks susp—"
"Dad! You do know what would happen if Eve finds out her father is alive?"

Eve's mind exploded. Carla had always said her father died when she was young. Even though she hadn't believed her, part of her always feared he was dead. She felt flooded with a cacophony of emotions; relief, anger, excitement and resentment were top of a long list.

Her dad was alive! She realised the reason for familiarity in the energy shape. This was her granddad. She had only seen him a couple of times growing up, but always had fond memories of him. Eve focused back on the conversation.

"He already knows Carla, he's probably on his way here eventually."
"Eventually? So where are they heading?"
"Look, I don't want to be in the middle of this. I told him I wouldn't tell you where he was heading."
"But what about Eve!"
"Isn't it right that she should see her father?"
"Why? So that she can know what it's like to live like a peasant? Living in that pigsty of a town?"

These Times

"Lana ain't that bad. It's full of character."
"And people with zero future. Here Eve can be our next great leader, with her powers she could rule the world."
"Is that what she wants? To rule?"
"She's young, she'll get the taste for it soon enough."
"Hmm, I can't help thinking this is your dream, not hers."
"So, it's my dream for her, is that so bad?"
"The odds are against you there, my girl. You were a teenager once, how did you feel back then when I tried to make you do something you didn't want to?"
"Oh, for god's sake, I don't need another lecture from an old soak like you. Just tell me what you know about Thomas!"
Wilf checked his watch.
"Well, I guess they should be out of harm's way by now. They were headed to the suburbs. They were taking Hector up there, or so they said."
"Hector? Not—"
"Yep, the very same. It's like a reunion of all your exes ain't it?"
"You think this is funny! What about the squirrels?"
"It's funny for me. Squirrels, they were erm, they were a strange couple of creatures. I don't think they are squirrels though, not really."
"What do you mean?"
"Well, I seen squirrels, large and small, but none like them. It was like they were borrowing a squirrel body

and stretching it over whatever form they actually are."

"What are they then? All the soldiers have been saying they're three-foot-high magical squirrels!"

"I dunno, I didn't recognise what was under the surface, it seemed like pure light. They're quite friendly you know, maybe you should invite them round for tea or somethin?"

"Very funny, but you have no idea what it's like to run a country in this day and age, do you?

These days I have to deal with psychic warriors, stealth agents, mutant hover marines, and to top it all, now I have sentient magical squirrels to worry about!"

"I agree! This place is getting dangerous. You need to protect Eve, take her to the Caverns."

"To be an underground prisoner?"

"Those Caverns are hardly a prison. The council chambers are some of the most comfortable places on Earth!"

"We'd still be prisoners."

"And what is this great tower anyway, if not a prison for the poor girl?"

"It's safe, that's what matters, and at least here she can see the sky, the sun."

"You're just avoiding being underground yourself. You always were claustrophobic."

"I hate being underground. But for your information I have already arranged for us to move to the Caverns."

"Great, so what are you doing about the squirrels and Thomas then?"

"I don't know. Aren't you supposed to be the one giving me fatherly wisdom?"

"I gave it to you: stay away from trouble and move to the Caverns."

"Useless, as always."

"Well, advice like that has served me pretty well. Do you see hordes of soldiers after me? Angry squirrels and ex-husbands chasing me down?"

"I bet mum would have helped if she was still alive."

"That ol' battle-axe would have been too busy sleeping with the butler, or the maid for that matter."

"Dad!"

"What? You know what your mother was like, she would—"

"I don't need you to bring that up now! Besides, haven't you heard of respecting the dead?"

"I'm not sayin anything I wouldn't say to her face if she were alive. If I was to speak respectfully that'd make me a complete hypocrite."

"Enough about mum, what are we going to do about Thomas?"

"I thought you didn't want advice from an old soak like me?"

"Dad, c'mon."

"Well, I'm off back to Lana. There's a pint of Gump that has my name on it, well I guess it's my name, hard to tell as they never clean the glasse—"

"DAD!"
Eve felt her mum's mind flash with rage and there was a flurry of motion in the room. She couldn't tell what had happened but she had a feeling her mum was being restrained by a force that seemed to be coming from her grandad.

"Listen up my dear, I love you but if you throw anythin like that at me again I swear I'll strip you of your powers and dump you right in the middle of your worst enemy's army, got it?"

"Yes Dad."

"Good." Eve felt the power in the room subside.

"Right, well I'll be off then. Take my advice Carla, stop this nonsense and buggering about with other countries. If you don't ever talk to Thomas about your daughter, which I think you should, then at least have a happy life with Eve."

"You really think I should talk to him?"

"I do."

"Do you think he'll ever forgive me?"

"Honestly, no. There's no way he can forgive what you did to him, but at least Eve would see her father. This is about Eve, not you two. Why are you so set against her having that human connection with her dad? It's starving her of love, and what for?"

"But I was doing the best—"

"It don't matter what you thought back then, it was wrong and you know it. All you can do now is say sorry and move on, maybe one day he might understand."

"You think?"

"Possibly, but you have robbed him of several years with his daughter and told him some hideous lies."

Eve's mind spun, her dad had no idea she was still alive! She delved deeper into her mother's mind, she wanted answers. Eve was inside her thoughts. They were cold and selfish. Totally absorbed in her own life and feelings.

She looked deeper inside her mother and found only darkness. A vast cavern of shallow pools of shadow; the thoughts and dreams of a narcissist.

Eve felt like screaming, yelling at her mother to think of her, at least once. Consider how she has been affected her whole life by her choices. Right then, Eve felt so alone. It quickly turned to rage and it boiled inside her till she let out a piercing cry from her soul. The lift shook and the power to the controls flickered. Every alarm bell in the building seemed to be ringing again. Her mum had heard or felt her. She was terrified, even her grandad was panicking. They were both stunned by the impact of Eve's scream.

Eve's anger grew as the weight of unreleased emotions piled upon her pain. The lift cage rippled with electricity. The display, no longer displaying the floor number, glowed brightly with gibberish. The controls and display started to smoke. A loud pop and the display exploded. The lift continued to shake. Her rage exploded out through her, sending bolts of lighting from her in all directions. The lift popped, cracked and buzzed with the power coursing through it. The lift accelerated upwards, faster and faster. The passing of floors were a blur. She was approaching the top of the tower and the lift showed no signs of stopping. Emergency brakes screeched on, causing the cage to jerk and shudder, but still the lift showed no signs of slowing down. Eve's rage still engulfed her in violent energy.

There were only a few floors left to the top of the shaft.

The Suburbs

Hector and Thomas climbed up the final hill that marked the boundary to the Suburbs. As they walked, the sun was setting and casting golden rays through the trees. The last few hours had been long and tedious. They had walked up the grassy hills out of the valley and up to the steeper tree-covered slopes. Their legs ached and despite the beauty of the scenery and the setting sun, their spirits were low. They found it even more annoying that Yorik and Grace didn't seem to tire at all. They continued to scamper about with a seemingly inexhaustible supply of energy.
"Have they always been like this?" asked Hector.
"Can't say I've had experience with giant squirrels, have you?"
"Surprisingly not."
"There's something more to them than meets the eye though."
Hector's eyebrows raised so high on his forehead that they almost reached his hairline.
"What makes you think that then? The shape-shifting? The talking?"
Thomas looked sideward at Hector, unsure whether to hit him or laugh.
"I mean all of that, plus I don't get the way Wilf back there talked about them. It was as if they weren't really squirrels."

"Yeah, he did seem to find something amusing about them. In my mind though, either we are traveling with talking, magical squirrels, or we're traveling with talking magical beings. Either way, we're involved with something bigger than we have ever seen before."

"True I guess. But you're still free to go if you want to, you know? I'm only staying with these creatures as they seem to want to get Eve away from Carla almost as much as me."

"I know, Tom. Believe me, if I didn't want to be here, I wouldn't be. I guess I feel it's better hanging around with magical squirrels than trying to hide from the search parties by myself."

Thomas looked at Hector, it seemed the last day had been hard on him. His once clean and smart clothes were now looking scruffy, worn, and dirty. His styled hair was disheveled with an obvious flick that refused to lie down.

"Yeah, you don't exactly seem like the outlaw type. What did you do anyway?"

"Um, I haven't worked in years. I have been looking after my wife. Funny, I can't even remember how long to be honest."

"But what did you used to do before that?"

"I used to be a programmer."

"A what?"

"Programmer. I used to write protocols for all the robots and automated stuff."

"People did that? I thought the robots just created themselves and looked after each other?"

"They do now. That's why they got rid of me and sent me out to Halmington. I was put on the maintenance crew that serviced the older droids."

"Sent to Halmington? Where did you live before that?"

"Burnim."

Their conversation fell away as they crested the hill and the Suburbs lay stretched out in a valley below them. The trees came to an abrupt stop a little past the top of the hill; it appeared as if they had been deliberately cut back. The valley was wide and shallow. On the other side of it the trees had also been cut back in a similar fashion. In the middle of the valley, a huge circle ringed with fences and barbed wire dominated the valley floor. At the edges of the circle the houses looked modern and comfortable. The houses and other buildings seemed to become more ramshackle the closer to the circle's center they were. However, what took their breath away was what they saw in the very middle of it.

In the very center of the circle a large pad of tarmac had been built. Currently, hovering above it, a cumbersome looking craft was slowly lowering itself onto the pad. It eased itself down and the doors opened. From the dark shadows of the ship's interior several figures stepped out. At this distance they could see something wasn't right with the figures but they couldn't make out quite what it was. They just didn't seem human. Hector and Thomas caught up with Yorik and Grace. They stood at the edge of the trees watching rows of people being shoved aboard the craft. A few of them resisted but were quickly silenced by a flash of light from one of the strange figures.

"Now I get why Wilf told us to approach from off the path," mumbled Hector.

"The preparation centers," Yorik said.

"The what? I thought this was the Suburbs? Where were people taken to retire?" asked Thomas.

"That's what they want you to believe. That way you won't put up a fight when it's your turn," answered Grace.

"Turn for what? Where are those people going? Why does it look like a prison?"

"It is a kind of prison. Except it's more like a kind of holding camp really. You see those people are being taken to— oh crap, RUN!"

"What?"

The squirrels disappeared in a flash. Thomas looked over to see the ominous floating orb of a drone zoom into view. It raced from behind the trees on the right to a few feet in front of them. The sleek metallic body glowed with angry red lights. It appeared to be scanning them.

Suddenly, a bright yellow light pulsed from a point in the center of its body. After the first couple of flashes, Thomas and Hector felt dizzy. The next few they felt drowsy. It flashed again and they passed out.

Grace and Yorik hid behind a nearby tree. They had looked away when the pulsing light had started. They knew the technology behind the light flashes and what it did to the mind.

"What now? Should we shut it down?" asked Grace.

"I don't think that would be a good idea, it might alert the whole security force and we'd never leave this valley."

"So, what should we do then? We can't leave them there; we need the useless idiots!"

"We'll wait till they have placed them in the camp, then we'll break them out. They should be done by nightfall."

"Won't that get all the alarms going?"

"No, they won't be expecting us. They built it to keep people in, not to keep people out."

"Hm, let's hope they're not in the 'ready meal' sector."

Exit Strategy

Carla walked along the spotless and highly polished corridor. She passed the remnants of the lift shaft and headed straight through two large opulently decorated doors that would have usually dominated the space.
"What did you do Eve?" she asked, calmly.
Eve was lounging on a sumptuously soft-looking sofa, trying her hardest to not look like she was deliberately lounging.
"What do you mean?" she replied meekly.
"The laboratory? The alarms?" Your shockwave that nearly blinded us, I mean me!"
"Us? Who were you with?" asked Eve leadingly.
"Doesn't matter. What did you do?"
"I dunno. I was watching the patients with the doctor, then the alarms went off and everything went a bit loopy."
"The Doctor told me you tried to teach the patients how to control their powers."
"Well, why did you ask me then? Were you trying to trick me deliberately?"
"Eve, I was giving you the chance to tell me the truth."
"I didn't mean to! I was just trying to help!" Eve's eyes teared up and she hid her face in her hands, she feigned a small sob.
Carla's hidden anger melted slightly, amused by her daughter's attempts at manipulation. She stood above

her looking uncomfortable, then stroked her hair as tenderly as she could muster.

"It's alright Eve, I understand. We've cleared it all up. I just want you to tell me the truth, that's all."

Eve coughed in the shock of hypocrisy from her statement, she sniffed and hid her tears in the soft material of Carla's dress.

"The shockwave, that was me." she said, muffled into the dress, if she had looked Eve would have seen her Mothers eyes roll in their greatest stretch ever.

"I saw you were with grandad, then I heard you say that dad was still alive." she continued.

"Ahh, I see," said Carla, stroking her daughter's hair awkwardly. She paused to collect her thoughts. "You see Eve, when people get old, like your granddad, they sometimes see things that aren't there."

"His mind seemed clear and fresh to me!"

"He's just sick, that's all. It's his mind's way of remembering things that gets jumbled up sometimes."

"But what he said doesn't make sense, why would he say that?"

"I know it's hard to understand Eve, but it's not your grandad talking, not really. It's like he's two people, the one that loves you and remembers every year you grew up in crystal clarity. Then there's the other grandad, he's like a child. He is confused and lost most of the time. Memories to him are like listening to a crowd of shouting people that he can't see. His thoughts and memories get all jumbled up. Even the way you see his mind, it doesn't reflect the inner turmoil."

Eve pulled away and looked up at her Mother. She realised then her mother had no idea how her powers worked and she obviously didn't have the same ones she did. She never saw "the mind", she saw the energy well that a soul emanated. Inner turmoil was the easiest thing to spot. More lies she thought. Then, torn between appreciating the unusual and uncomfortable affection Carla was showing her and wanting to scream at her for lying, she hugged her again.

"Will he get better?"

"Probably not Eve. I'm afraid if anything he will get worse."

"Can't we help him get better? We can do loads of stuff that others can't!"

"I know we can. Sometimes things just happen, things that are meant to happen, and we shouldn't try to change them."

"But grandad—"

"Eve, you need to be a grownup for me here, please try to understand."

Eve sat back on the sofa sulkily and crossed her arms.

"Some things have happened." she continued, "It looks like we'll need to move."

"Move? Where?"

"A place called The Caverns, it's where the most influential and powerful people in the country are living."

"Why are we moving there?"

"A few reasons, the main one is that it is safe there. There are some people who want to hurt us, but they won't be able to."

"Fine. Beats this lifeless tower anyway."

"It's not that bad. But I imagine you'll love it there. It's full of people like us and it's built into large caves and caverns carved into the rock."

"It's below the ground?"

"That's right, one of the many things that make it so safe."

"No windows? No garden?"

"They have some gardens on the upper levels, but people mostly stay below ground. They have parks and even waterfalls down there."

"Hmm. Sounds like another place to be trapped."

Preparation Station Theta

Thomas woke to the sound of chirping birds and the babbling, of what he imagined to be, a small stream. His eyes slowly adjusted to the dim light and he found that he was in a very opulently decorated bedroom. Above him the ceiling was moving. It looked as if he was staring up at the sky from a forest floor, tall trees arched above his head. He noticed the walls were moving as well; the walls displayed an area of the forest near his old family home. It was the area he grew up around. The ceiling above him changed subtly from the glow of dawn to the deep dark blue of a mid-morning summer's day. The forest scene projected on the walls around him grew lighter and was speckled with sunshine. Thomas felt peculiar. He didn't know where he was or why he was here. He wasn't even sure of his name. He did have one overriding feeling though, he felt very calm.

Thomas tried to remember what had happened the day before, but for the life of him, he had no idea at all, not even the vaguest glimmer of a memory. Even this thought didn't interrupt his calmness. Thomas laid back on his bed and stared at the blue sky on the ceiling above him. He watched the accelerated passing of time with detached bemusement. The sun rose into his vision. The light wasn't painful to look at. It wasn't as intense as the morning sun in reality. This light made him feel like he needed to get up and do

something. He shuffled to the edge of the luxuriously soft bed and swung his feet down onto a thick warm carpeted floor. Thomas stood up and walked through the only door. He still had no idea where he was or even who he was. However, he still felt strangely calm about it. Thomas wondered why he wasn't feeling more anxious, but that feeling too, quickly passed.
In the next room there were two comfortable sofas arranged opposite each other. A man was seated on one of them. He had a bemused smile on his face. Thomas thought the man's face looked familiar, but again, his memories remained foggy.
"Hello," said Thomas.
"Hi."
"You live here?"
"I'm not sure, I think so. I just woke up and I can't seem to remember anything."
"I can't either! Isn't that funny? I wonder where we are?"
"Doesn't seem like a bad place though, I guess. My room is pretty amazing, well, I'm guessing it's my room."
"Yeah? The forest is a nice touch." smiled Thomas.
"Forest?"
"The room, yours is like being in a forest too, right?"
"No." he said gently, shaking his head. "Mine is how I imagine energy connections flow between cities, between people, between souls. Bright blue pulses of intense energy being sent back and forth. It's like I can

see the luminous world pulse with life around me. It's beautiful."

Thomas sat down on the sofa opposite the man. The cushions wrapped around him and he felt very comfortable.

"What's your name?" asked Thomas.

"Funny you should ask, I was just trying to remember, I think it starts with an H."

"An H? Hubert?"

"No."

"Henry?"

"I think it's a bit like that."

"Like Henry, hmm. Well there's Henly, Hect—"

"Hector. That sounds familiar."

"Well, Hector it is for now."

"I can't believe I forgot my own name," Hector said smiling. "What's yours anyway?"

"Thomas. At least I think it is. Does it worry you that both our memories seem to be so bad?"

"It does, a little, but then everything is so comfortable here."

"Yeah, it is nice here."

"It certainly is nice."

Hector and Thomas sat in silence, staring at the blank wall, totally content. They sank into the sofas and drifted between realms of consciousness.

Yorik and Grace sat on a tree branch overlooking the circular complex below them. They had been here since yesterday evening.

"There, I think they took them into that building over there," said Grace.

"I can't make them out clearly. There's interference," replied Yorik, he was trying to sense the building Grace had pointed out.

"We haven't had a chance to teleport there. Can't you get a message to them?"

"No, I can't get past that interference either. We'll need to get down there on foot and break them out. No other way." replied Grace.

They looked at the horizon and the last rays of the glorious setting sun.

"It'll be another couple of hours before it's dark enough to attempt that."

"I hope they're okay down there."

"They'll be fine. They're in the Free-Range quarter." quipped Yorik.

"Must you call it that?"

"Well that's what it is! It's all to tenderise them, isn't it? It's those poor sods in the economy range I feel for. They get rammed in those tight cabins together, barely room to breathe."

"It's not our place to judge, we have horrors in our past too."

"I still can't believe the human leaders have let this happen! Even when we were outnumbered and on the brink of being wiped out, our elders never had made the deals they have."

"They're frightened. Fear does strange things to otherwise rational beings. Don't forget this species is a lot younger than ours."

Yorik looked at the complex of buildings below them. He watched some of the human captives walking drearily about one of the exercise yards.

"Do you think they'll make it?" asked Yorik.

"Thomas and Hector?"

"No," he sighed, "Humans."

"Oh. Well they have a reasonable chance if we can stop all this madness and get them to take our help."

"Have there been any updates?"

"No. We've caught up with them a little, but they had such a head start it wouldn't make that much of a difference."

"Are we still many years behind them?"

"Not as many as you might think, it's around ten now and it's still falling."

"You'll think the humans can hold on for that long?" asked Yorik.

"Well, it'll be a long ten years for them, but we can help them defend themselves. Provided they start working together. But if they keep up all this petty bickering and power play–" she stopped mid sentence to watch the magical beauty of the Sunsets' closing moments. As the light faded, she concluded: "They'll have no hope."

Hector and Thomas were roused from their peaceful thoughts by a soft, pleasant voice. It filled the air around them, it seemed to have no single source.
"Good morning residents, welcome to your new home. Would you like to eat? Would you like to exercise? The kitchen is fully stocked and a breakfast has been laid out for you on the floor above. You can also find a fully provisioned gymnasium there complete with a luxurious heated swimming pool and sauna facilities. We highly recommend that you eat well and exercise daily. Exercise keeps you healthy and happy. If you need anything, just press the blue section on any of the panels in any of the rooms. Good day."
A door to their left clicked, a panel that had been highlighted red, flicked to green and the friendly voice returned.
"Second story access now granted. Enjoy."
Hector looked at Thomas and they simultaneously shrugged their shoulders. Thomas stood up and opened the door that had just clicked. Behind it there was a flight of stairs that led up to another door. Thomas climbed the stairs and up to the door, Hector followed behind him. He opened the door at the top to reveal a large room that they were now in the middle of. The room had glass walls around the edge of the house that stretched from floor to ceiling. Above them the ceiling was also made of glass. There was a small stretch in front of them that was open to the sky above.

Below it a blue swimming pool stretched from one side of the house to the other. The rest of the room was behind glass partitions and filled with a variety of equipment. Thomas thought most of them looked like torture devices. In the very far corner section there was a small collection of kitchen units and a breakfast bar filled with sumptuous looking food.

"What's all this about then?" asked Thomas.

"For us to keep healthy and entertained I imagine," Hector replied.

"What?"

"This is all gym equipment isn't it?"

"Gym?"

"Yeah, gymnasium. Don't you know what that is?"

"No. You do?"

"Yeah, somehow I do. A gym is a place where you go to exercise."

"What? What do you mean 'a place you go to exercise'?"

"It's to keep you fit and healthy?"

"Why?"

"Why do you want to be fit and healthy?"

"No, why do you need a place to go and exercise?"

"You need to exercise somewhere."

"But don't you get that from just doing stuff every day?"

"Well, I guess, but for some reason I remember having to use one."

"What did you used to do then?"

Hector scratched the side of his head and stared into the distance.

"That's strange, I don't actually know. How about you?" he asked, turning to Thomas.

Thomas looked completely baffled as he searched his brain for any memories of his past.

"Nope, no idea either." He shrugged.

"Oh well, I guess it can't be that important then! Anyway, I'm going for a swim," said Hector.

"Hmm, I think I'll just look at the scenery for a while." Thomas flopped down onto a comfortable chair to his left. He lounged back and looked out through the glass wall to the beautiful countryside beyond. The illusion projected on the glass was so convincing that he didn't question it. Nor did he question how they appeared to be the only house for miles around. Outside the bright sunshine highlighted the rolling green hills with a fresh bright beauty.

Thomas sat there, his mind drifting around in a wasteland of empty thoughts, happy in the complete peace he found there. Hector had changed his clothes and was happily swimming back and forth in the narrow but long pool.

Thomas spotted a very large squirrel climbing over the glass wall in front of him. He felt he should be alarmed by its size but for some reason, he wasn't.

Never Underestimate a Squirrel

Carla scrambled over the shattered desk in her office trying to find the ringing phone. It was in a new hole in the wall. She wrenched it out and accepted the call. The screen on the wall flickered briefly to present the head and shoulders of Director William Jones, Head of Preparation Station Theta.

"What do you need Will? As you can see, this isn't the best of times."

"Sorry to interrupt, ma'am. We have just caught two people on the outskirts of our facility, matching the outlaws Hector and Thomas. Here's their mugshots." The director made some movements with his hand outside the view of him and two large profile pictures were projected onto the wall in front of Carla. Her jaw dropped in disbelief.

"Tell me, was there anything else with them?" she replied, feigning composure.

"Anything else?"

"Yes, like animals, larger than normal maybe?"

The Director squirmed uneasily.

"Well, now that you mention it, yes. I didn't want to say until we had it confirmed, but the drone that picked them up reported that there were two large squirrels with them. They disappeared as soon as the drone engaged."

"I need you to find those squirrels!"

"We're scouring the surrounding forest but haven't found a trace of them yet."

"Find them Will! Find them *now!*"

"Yes ma'am, we're doing everything we can." He answered nervously.

"Until you find them you are not doing enough."

"Yes ma'am."

"Where are Hector and Thomas?"

"We have them in the Luxury Preparation Accommodations."

"Tightly locked down, yes?"

"Yes, they are currently restricted to the house. They're under deep mind control. We've had them physically tranquilized and the dose of mood inhibitors is the most they can safely take."

"And you're monitoring them, closely?"

"Yes, the usual surveillance, plus we have a perimeter detail that is constantly monitoring the outside."

"Have another three units assigned to it. I want each side of that house under non-stop surveillance."

"What are you expecting to happen? Thomas and Hector are only a couple of drifters aren't they?"

"As much as I hate to say it, those drifters are more important than you could possibly imagine."

"Oh, and the squirrels?"

"If I'm right those squirrels will be back to get Thomas and Hector. They could be a bigger problem than you take them for, mark my words. Be ready with every anti-psionic weaponry you have. I need them to capture Will." Carla leaned closer to the screen and stared into William's eyes. "I cannot express how important this is Will, I need them back here in the tower, all of them. When you have them, contact me and we'll arrange transport."

"Yes Ma'am."

"I'm rearranging my plans till this is dealt with. Oh, and Will."

"Yes?"

"I'm sure I don't need to remind you if you fail me . . ." The Director twitched and shifted uneasily again, remembering his predecessor's fate.

"Yes ma'am, I understand."

Follow My Lead

Despite the appearance of a disturbingly large squirrel, Thomas still felt very calm. The squirrel was now climbing clumsily up the glass wall. It reached the glass ceiling and heaved its body up. It turned to the glass ceiling, now beneath it, and started to scratch. A few ear piercing scrapes later, the squirrel fell through the ceiling, accompanied by splintering glass. Thomas still felt very calm. He even remained peaceful when another slightly smaller, but still disturbingly large, squirrel appeared and followed the path of the other. How could he feel agitation in this peaceful place? He pondered as the second squirrel assisted the other in getting back up. It looked a little dazed. Thomas felt an artificial euphoria robe him in bliss as he continued to lounge in his reclining chair. He chuckled to himself when those same two squirrels appeared to walk through the glass partition between him and the pool area. He felt like he should be worried that these odd events were happening and that he should be even more concerned that they weren't actually bothering him at all.
"Thomas!" said the largest furry creature.
"Hi, I'm Thomas. Who are you?"
"Just an idea, but how about we try escaping first?" said the smaller one.
"Escape what?" asked Thomas.
"Here! This place."

"Oh, why?" asked Thomas, completely confused.
The larger squirrel hopped over to Thomas with surprising agility. It jumped onto his lap and he winced with the large weight of the giant furball. The beady-eyed creature looked deep into his eyes.
"Bugger. They've wiped him. Probably controlling his emotional state as we speak." The squirrel said looking back to the other. He hopped down from Thomas's lap.
"Permanent wipe?" asked the smaller squirrel.
"I don't think it's permanent, more like the memories are hidden or suppressed."
"Should I try to get them back?"
"Not now, not in this place. We need to get them out of here."
"Who are you?" Thomas asked again.
"We're, ah, friends, here to help you. I'm Yorik, this is Grace," said the smaller squirrel.
"Why do I have the feeling that you shouldn't be able to talk? And that you are somehow familiar?"
"It's a long story. Let us tell you on the way out of here."
"Why? Are we leaving?"
"You're not safe here!" said Yorik.
"Why isn't it . . . it . . . safe . . ." Thomas mumbled. His chin dropped to his chest.
"We need to . . . Hang on, Thomas? THOMAS?" Yorik hopped onto Thomas' lap and shook his shoulders.

Grace looked over to the pool. Hector had stopped swimming and was climbing out of the pool. He stood up and his eyes glazed over.

"Hector? Are you ok?"

"Hmmm," he replied and started to lie down on his back. As soon as he lay his head gently on the floor, his eyes closed.

"Hector?"

"Oh crap! They're onto us. Follow my lead," said Grace. She fell to the floor and shut her eyes.

"What?" asked Yorik. "Oh! I see!" and fell awkwardly to the floor, clamping his eyes shut.

Yorik reached out with his presence to contact Grace. *What's going on?* He asked the mental presence of Grace.

They're coming, they must have set a trap for us.

But why are we giving in?

If we wait, we will probably be taken to Carla.

Oh! But won't they sense the psychic weapon or whatever they used, hasn't worked on us? Asked Yorik.

Carla probably will, but just use your shielding. She won't know what we are and presume she can't read us, hopefully.

Hopefully? How long do we have to lie here then?

Not long, I think they'll monitor us for a while to make sure we have really been knocked out. But how will we know when it's safe again? Asked Yorik.

Use your mind sight.

Do you remember how to do that?

Mind sight! That was in our basic training. Do you remember? Yorik deflected.

Of course. Grace replied.

You know I feel that you've forgotten right? You do know how all this works right? Asked Grace, *How did he get assigned to this mission?* she asked herself.

*Well, as I remember I was chosen for my empathy, something I vaguely remember you having a problem with.*Yorik answered.

I don't know what you mean, we should really stay sil –

Ah yes, that's it, I believe it was your mission on the planet Trappist when they realised how hopeless you were?

I wouldn't say hopeless exactly. Besides, I don't really recall.

Oh, I think you do. I don't think there's ever been a scouting party yet that has come close to causing such calamity or even approaching your kill count.

I didn't kill them! Grace's mental voice boomed in Yorick's head.

No, no, you're right there. It was more of an accidental slaughter. What was it you did again?

I just said that their pets were a little annoying!

That's right, that's all you said. And what did they end up doing?

There was a long pause, then eventually, through the mental communication plane, the sheepish thought pattern of Yorik stumbled forth.

They killed them all.

Yes, that's right, I remember now! Killed them all, why did they do that?

I can read your thoughts, you know! I can tell that you remember all this.

I don't know what you mean. Grace snapped.

They thought we were gods and that we would be unhappy unless they wiped their pets out.
Oh yes, and why didn't you spot that they would treat us like gods?
Yorik mentally sighed at Grace.
The elders said I lacked empathy.
Exactly! Hence, why I'm here.
Yay for us. Very good, you've had your fun, let's just be silent now. Thought Grace.
Just one last thing. The buzzing presence of Yorik asked.
I never heard what happened to them. Did we recreate their pets for them?
Yorik felt a ripple of low frequency energy flow through him, his question had brought some bad feelings back for Grace. It was a shadow cast from a place of deep pain and regret.
No, we didn't have time to synthesize any.
Really? Why?
They all died.
What! Grace felt genuine shock from the comment.
Apparently, their pets weren't just pets. They were living in symbiosis with them. The creatures actually groomed their fur and ate all of the parasites they had on them. One of those parasites was quite a nasty flesh eating one. Unabated, they wiped out the whole species within a couple of days.
You wiped out a whole species of sentient beings? Because you didn't like their pets?
Yeah, but there is an argument that if they didn't know the little creatures were keeping them alive, they would have wiped them out by accident one day anyway.

Is that right?
Shut up Yorik, they'll be scanning for us soon. Keep quiet even here.

The squirrels laid there in complete silence as several soldiers crept up the stairs. Although Yorik could sense them and read their minds, he couldn't physically see them. He had forgotten how to use the mind to see the world around him. This was never interesting for him in basic training. He liked seeing the energy shapes of other beings and how they worked, how to connect with them, and how to understand their complicated colours. He vaguely remembered the mind sight training; it had something to do with using your thought projection like an echo or something, but he couldn't remember how it worked.

He didn't see the soldiers as they climbed the stairs, he was blissfully unaware of their menacing black-red uniforms and the laser rifles each of them held. He could however, look into their minds and see the world as one of them. He jumped into the mind of the last in through the door and watched as they broke from their creeping pose. They stormed the room and secured it. He saw his own body on the ground as the soldier swept across the room, covering the rear of his squad. Yorik watched the lead guard kick his body, then Grace's. When they seemed convinced the squirrels weren't going to move, they lowered their rifles.

The lead soldier spoke through his head-mounted mic. "The psych bomb worked, they're out cold. Are we clear to extract?"

There was a pause while he listened to the response. "Roger, move out to rendezvous point alpha now."

He nodded at his team and they picked up the bodies of Yorik, Grace, Thomas, and Hector. They slung the bodies over their shoulders and then carried them down the stairs and out through the front door.

Outside the street was a bleak contrast to the opulent interior. The houses were dilapidated, as if they were built from a bygone era. The street itself was a mud bath. Floating just above the surface of the street a bulky well-worn van hovered waiting for them. The guards threw the bodies into the back of the van and climbed in after them. The leader closed the doors and climbed into the front. The van rose slightly into the air and hurtled off down the street.

"Back to the tower. Quickly! The last thing we need is any of this lot waking up." the leader said to the driver.

Yorik watched the streets race by then quickly turn into countryside. Trees flew past the windows. Eventually they seemed to be heading straight into a gigantic stone wall that cut across the countryside. As the wall rose in front of them cutting out the skyline, they showed no sign of slowing down. Grace jumped to see the eyes of the driver. She could make out a small black hole in front of them. As they headed towards it, she saw the hole grow into a large tunnel.

Within seconds they had passed into it. The tunnel was black, unlit, cut off from any sunlight. The van sped deeper into the solid rock until suddenly, Grace felt a sharp pain in her head and she lost the connection with the soldier. Everything was black.

Welcome to the Tower

Thomas opened his eyes and immediately regretted it. White light flooded his eyeballs and pierced his brain. He clamped his eyelids shut and when he felt the giant spots in his vision subside, he opened them very cautiously. As his eyes adjusted, he began to make out various shapes moving around the room. Eventually he opened his eyes fully but everything was still so very white and so very bright.

He was lying on his back in some kind of laboratory. His arms and legs were restrained by bindings he couldn't see. Looking to his left he could see the others were lying on beds similar to his. The bodies of the large squirrels looked even more surreal as they were stretched over the shiny metal tables. He heard someone enter the room behind him.

"Is he awake yet?" said the newcomer. He couldn't see who it was, but the voice was unnervingly familiar.

"Thomas has just woken up. The others are still drifting."

Steps rounded his table then a face peered over the top, upside down to him.

"Hullo, Tom."

"Carla!"

"Tom. Didn't I leave you in that turd of a village?"

Thomas felt the anger ignite inside him burn with an uncontrollable ferocity. His arms and legs flailed against the bindings.

"You lying cow! I know you set it all up, set me up! Where's Eve?"

"What? What are you talking about?"

"I know what you did! You took our daughter you sick–."

"I haven't the faintest idea who you've been listening to, but I have no idea what you mean about Eve. I want us to be friends, Tom. In fact, I'm here to help you."

"Don't lie to me! Your guard told me everything!"

"Oh. That's right! Of course I always tell dark secrets to my guards. You cretin."

"He told me he was your escort to the Caverns!"

"I don't get involved with the details of my security team! I'm far too busy to worry about that."

"He knew you."

"Anyone can claim that!"

"But they wouldn't say it directly to your face though, would they?"

"Er. I guess not. What do you mean?" Carla asked a little nervously.

"The guard thought I was you."

"What?"

"I have this ability to change into whatever I like. I was changed to be like you."

"Oh, fascinating." she said, studying Thomas with a renewed interest. "You can shape shift then? Who taught you that?"

"Where is Eve?"

Carla summoned a white-coated assistant.

He approached Thomas's bed and prepared a syringe of liquid. When he had finished, he grabbed Thomas's arm and glanced up at Carla. The syringe was poised, awaiting her signal.

Carla took a deep breath and looked at Thomas. She seemed to be weighing her chances of getting away with more lies or whether to just come clean. At last, she sighed.

"Safe, she's somewhere very safe."

"Where?"

"You won't find her, and please don't try. She's happy where she is and she's much better off than if she'd have stayed with you!"

"How can you say that! How dare you take my daughter away from me! I'll–" Carla nodded to the assistant and he sank the needle into Thomas's vein, he pressed the plunger on the syringe.

"Ow! What the h—"

"It's just a sedative, to help you calm down and get some rest," answered the assistant.

"Thomas, Eve is exceptionally talented. She needed the education that only the city could provide. Now she is gaining control of her powers, Eve will be vital in saving the world."

"I'll— l— l ffff-in-dd hh errrr!" slurred Thomas, rapidly losing consciousness.

"What do you want us to do with them? He's not the only one beginning to wake up and we can't keep them all permanently sedated."

These Times

Carla ran her delicate hands through her dyed blonde hair and scratched at her scalp. Thomas appearing was bad enough, Hector being with him was even worse. Yet she hadn't the heart to kill them outright, they all had history. Still, she could do the next best thing without the guilt of directly killing them.

"Perform the procedures on Hector and Thomas. Put them in the restricted ward and keep an eye on them. This one could be a real problem when he wakes up." Carla said, pointing to the slumbering body of her ex-husband. "Sounds like he already has some abilities. He could be dangerous."

"Ma'am?"

"He's already part way down the rabbit hole, the next procedure will probably send his abilities into overdrive!"

"Down the rabbit hole?"

Carla chuckled to herself. "An ancient literary reference. He's traveling between worlds, between the slumbering one of ignorant bliss he knew and this one of being awake, with all its dangerous powers. Make sure the ward has the shielding systems on full power."

"Yes ma'am, and what about the squirrels?"

"Put them in an isolation chamber. And put every restraining shield generator and security measure we can spare on it."

Thomas opened his eyes. His brain felt foggy but he was sure he was in a completely different room. This room was more like a hospital ward than the mad biology lab he had first woken up in. There was another bed opposite his, Hector was sleeping in it. The windows of the room and the entrance to the ward was sealed with a translucent barrier that shimmered ever so slightly. On the other side of the barrier to the ward Thomas could just make out the blurred outlines of several people in white coats. They walked back and forth between what he guessed was monitoring equipment. Although the details were lost and muffled, he could hear them chattering excitedly to each other.

He heard Hector groan as he regained consciousness.

"Hector," croaked Thomas, making him realise how dry his throat was.

"Hmmm, where are we?" Hector shuffled in his bed till he was sitting upright. "Why are we in a hospital?"

"I'm not sure."

"The last thing I can remember is that drone—"

"Yeah, it all seems to have gone black from there for me too. But I do remember waking up in a lab somewhere, Carla was there."

"Carla?"

"Gentlemen." Carla's voice resonated from a hidden speaker system. The image of her flickered onto a screen that was descending from the ceiling. She stood by the entrance to the ward and was speaking into a small glass object. "I understand you might be confused, that's entirely natural and only slightly worrying for your health."

"What have you done now, Carla?" spat Thomas.

"Hector, it's been a long time," she said, blatantly ignoring Thomas.

"Carla," Hector said in a cold emotionless voice.

"You know each other!" cried Thomas.

"We met a long while ago, before we met Tom."

"Why didn't you say that before?" Thomas asked Hector.

"I wasn't sure it was the same Carla that I knew. I suspected it, but didn't want it to be true."

"Eh?"

"She's the one who killed my wife!" Hector seethed.

"What!" cried Thomas.

"Now, now Hector. That's a wild accusation! You have no reason to believe it was me!"

"Then what were you doing in Halmington that day? The same day you weirdly touched her she fell gravely ill! You did something to her didn't you?"

"I'd just left Tom, I was traveling. I didn't even know you had settled there. I was just trying to be friendly."

"You went to see him after making me think Eve was dead? You left Eve alone?"

"No, they took her away at first. They needed to run tests and analyse the best way to teach her. I needed time to get my head straight too; it was the best for all of us."

"YOU needed time?"

"Thomas look, I was just trying to—"

"Why did you have to kill them?" cried Hector, cutting across Carla.

"Hector, I'm sorry about your family but I had absolutely nothing to do with it."

"And how am I supposed to believe you? After all you've done!"

"I'll admit I have done many bad things to you Hector, but why would I kill your family?"

"Because you're an evil witch who can't stand seeing anyone happy!"

The venom in Hector's words hit the room like a wave of stagnant water, leaving nothing but an awkward silence in its wake.

"What have you done to us then?" asked Thomas, eventually breaking the silence.

"Nothing. Well, I have done you both a great favour."

"What have you done?" repeated Thomas.

"We ran some procedures on you and we've opened your minds."

"What the hell does that mean?"

"She means she's experimented on us and flooded our brains with enhancers," answered Hector.

"What? Is that good then? I presume it is, isn't it? Now we can break out of this place?"

"Well, Hector is right, but you're not Thomas. See, the room is shielded and none of the other subjects lasted

long enough to work their new powers let alone break free."
"What?" cried Thomas again.
"If she's using the same experiments she did in the past. The people she experimented on didn't last long after the operation."
"Didn't last long? How long is that?"
"A long time ago I used to work in a lab like this. There are several all over the city. All the experiments were about enhancing the brain, and yeah, their heads, they kind of . . ."
"Exploded!" finished Carla. "You should have seen it, like fireworks in a slaughterhouse! Let's hope Hector goes first, Tom, then you'll be able to see it yourself!"
"Why the hell would you do this to us?"
"Research. It's always good to get more data."
"You're still hiding parts of your mind though," Hector said. "There's another reason."
"It's the shielding. It only lets in what I want it to. You're picking up that resistance I imagine."
"I'm going to get out Carla, and I'll—"
"Yeah, yeah, this isn't the first time we've done this. Let's just skip the hollow threats, I really don't have time for it." The speaker system and screen abruptly clicked off.
"What a cow! I knew she was twisted, but wow!" said Thomas.
"What are we going to do? Seeing as our heads could explode any minute!" asked Hector.

"Do you reckon all of it was for real? Or is she messing with us? She used to love doing that."

"I don't know, but I imagine a bit of both. She did love to play mind games and terrorising people. But some of the experiments they used to do here did end up with people exploding."

"Great. How long have we got then?"

"Hard to tell, some barely lasted an hour, others survived days. Depends on how your body takes to the serum."

"Did all of them explode?"

"No, only most of them actually exploded I think."

"Not the best of odds then," concluded Thomas.

Close Quarters

On the other side of the tower from Hector and Thomas, Grace and Yorik were pacing back and forth in a small windowless room. The room was barely big enough for their two beds.

They walked on their hind legs like humans, except they weren't. These two giant squirrels looked completely out of place. If their fur wasn't quite so real and every atom of their bodies wasn't arranged in a squirrel form, you would swear you were watching a couple of drunks in Halloween costumes.

At first, they had started out politely letting each other pass. The politeness had quickly eroded to passing grunts as they waited for the other to move out of their way. This in turn, quickly led to a race condition where each would quicken their pace ever-so-slightly to reach the middle first. However, as their speed increased this led to even more frustration as they had to pass more often. It was only a matter of time before one of them broke.

"WOULD YOU SIT DOWN FOR–!"

"SOD YOU YORIK! WHY SHOULD I BE THE ONE TO SIT DOWN!""

"LOOK!" he started, then lowered his voice, "This is a ridiculously small room, why can't we just bust out of here?"

"We've been through this. If we rescue them, they'll always rely on us to save them. They need to feel like they have the power, that they saved us."
"But why?"
"They need to feel the responsibility of their own power, for confidence if nothing else."
"So it's either wait and let them save us, or we'll need to fake our own deaths to let them deal with Carla?"
"Personally, I'd rather stick around Yorik."
"I don't get why they just can't learn to use their powers alongside ours?"
"Human psychology, Yorik. If they think there's a more advanced protective power, they'll rely on it."
"But I thought they did that alpha dominance thing?"
"They do, but it'll take years before they'll feel confident enough to challenge us. They need to find their strength now."
"Fine, we'll stay here till they get us. But could you at least keep the same pace so you don't keep blocking the way!"
"I'm blocking the way?"
"Yes."
"How can you accuse me of that?"
Yorik leaned into Grace's personal space, his face was so close his whiskers tickled Grace's nose.
"Because you keep getting in *my* way!"
"I think you'll find that you are blocking the way," Grace said as she shoved Yorik so hard he fell

backward. His head banged against the wall as he hit the ground.

Immediately, Yorik was back on his feet and shoved Grace back even harder. Grace was ready for it and although she stumbled back, she quickly rebalanced her weight and punched Yorik in the face.

Yorik yelped and staggered backward, clasping his paw to his eye.

"Why you—" Yorik wiped his eye then held his paw out. The air quivered as he charged it with an electric blue haze. He sent it flowing toward Grace and a shockwave crashed into her. Grace was flung against the back wall.

"Right. It's like that is it?" said Grace standing back up. Grace held out an opened paw. As she closed it, every object in the room not anchored down rose into the air. She turned her arm over and made a shoving gesture. All the objects flew at a phenomenal speed towards Yorik.

Sorry?

Carla waved her hand in front of the controls of the aircar door and the expertly machined, highly polished doors silently slid closed. Eve's acting sad face, partially occluded by the tinted glass, looked forlornly back at her. Carla waved and smiled. She mouthed the words "I'll be with you soon."

Eve stared back at her and waved with the unenthusiastic half-committal that only teenagers can seem to master. Despite this, Carla kept her energetic wave going as long as she could. She watched the aircar rise and float westwards into the setting sun. Carla walked back through the roof access door and sighed with relief. It had been a long tough battle getting Eve to go. She had been very suspicious. It had taken all of her will to resist Eve's mind probe but somehow, she had held out. Eve was getting stronger and more accomplished every time she tried to read her mind. One day soon she knew there would be nothing she could do to stop her from knowing every thought in her head. That was quite worrying.

Carla had never told her the truth about Thomas. She thought it was the right thing to do when she left him. Now, years later, it was those decisions that weighed heavily on her. She knew it had been right to leave, but perhaps with the wisdom she carried today, she would have chosen a better way to do it. However, what was done was done and her plan rolled ever onward. Ever mutating to try and stop it all from unraveling.

She entered the lift at the end of the corridor and rode it down all the way to the laboratories. Carla wondered if Thomas or Hector would actually be killed by the experiment. She half hoped they wouldn't. Carla had never realised this before but she had missed Thomas. He was a bit naïve and lacked finesse but she had loved him once.

She knew Thomas would hate her forever now he knew the truth, there was zero chance they could ever be together again. She had stolen Eve from him and betrayed him in unimaginable ways, not to mention making him think his daughter had died.

The squirrels intrigued her too. She had heard of the 'spirit' that guarded the forest, a strange talking tree by all accounts. Carla had never heard of enlarged squirrels though. She was very interested in their particular vent of magic. It was quite different from the type she had learnt and the type her experimenting with humans produced. With humans it was more a heightening of brain functions and letting science do the rest through manipulations of energy and matter. But the squirrels and the tree creature had quite a different physiology. With them it seemed the magic was ingrained in their bodies. Every cell had an ability to focus and manipulate not only energy, but other dimensions too. She believed, whilst being secretly mocked by the scientists in the laboratory, that they could travel vast distances instantaneously, She secretly hoped they could travel through time.

Carla stepped out of the lift and onto the laboratories corridor. She headed towards the observation ward. She was quite surprised to see Thomas and Hector working together and throwing any piece of furniture they could at the shielded walls. The lab technicians were nowhere to be seen.

"Gentleman! What seems to be the problem?" she asked.

"We are not going to sit here and wait for ourselves to explode!" gasped Hector, out of breath from the exertion.

"We will get out of here Carla, and I'm going to kill you," spat Thomas. He grabbed one of the pieces of monitoring equipment, wrenched it free, and hurled it against the shimmering field she stood behind.

"Your time would be much better spent learning to use the powers we have just given you. At least you'd have some fun before you exploded."

"How could you do this to us? To Eve? How can you try to kill me now?"

Carla looked into Thomas's enraged eyes through the monitors, she felt that twinge she got when emotions were trying to overwhelm her, she looked down at her feet.

"I was forced to by the Council. They needed a young face, a more powerful person for their tasks, they wanted Eve. They gave me powers and offered me a position too, providing I let them use Eve."

"The Council?"

"Yes, it's made up of the leaders of the civilised world."

"You made a deal using our daughter's life? And you made me think she was dead?"

"The Council stipulated the outside world should believe Eve had died. Besides, what would I have said? What would you have said to a proposition like that?"

"You could have talked to me! We could have worked something out! But you made me think Eve died and then you left me."

"It wasn't by my choice that I led you to believe those things. I really hated that part. Now however, the Council is under my control and I can choose a new advisor, I can choose to be with whoever I want."

"WHAT HAVE YOU DONE WITH EVE?" yelled Thomas.

"Nothing, she is quite safe. I have moved her to the Council headquarters. She is in the safest place on this planet."

"Where is she?"

"If she has been sent to the headquarters, it means she is in the Caverns of Western Stoll," answered Hector.

"How do you know that Hector?" asked Thomas.

"Working in the labs we had to send all our reports there. Everyone used to talk about the place. The best-known worst kept secret."

"Thomas, I am really sorry about Eve, about everything. I'm sorry about what I did to you and if I could, I would give anything to save you that pain. We needed Eve to change the world for the better. Eve was, and is, essential to the survival of the human race."

"What?" they chorused.

It was at that moment the cold calculating part of Carla's mind hatched a plan. She knew how she could keep them busy while Eve was locked down and have some fun with them at the same time.

All in the Mind

Thomas was surrounded by darkness. A small pinprick of light appeared in front of him. Slowly the light grew until the darkness around him dissolved into a beautiful spring morning. He was standing in front of his old home, the one he had shared with Carla many years ago. Through the windows he could see a younger version of Carla moving semi-dressed around the house. He noticed another version of herself leaning against a tree near him.
"What's all this about? Are you trying to trick me again? Is this a dream?" Thomas asked.
"This is like a waking dream, you're still alive and awake in the real world, well, the lab. This is just my memories, projected into your mind. I thought it would do you good to see the past. The bits you might have missed."
"Parts I missed?"
"Yes, the parts that happened when you weren't there. When things happened that I'm ashamed of."
"You're ashamed of? I'm not sure I want to see this. What's the point in dredging up the past?"
"You need to see what I could never bring myself to tell you. The truth behind why I wanted to escape."
"The truth?"
"Yes, just watch."
Suddenly the front door burst open and Carla appeared, she looked furtively up and down the street.

Once she was sure there was no one watching she ushered out a half-dressed man. Thomas couldn't believe his eyes. It was Hector. As Hector fastened his trousers and buttoned his shirt, he could overhear them talking.

"—but why so suddenly? Didn't you know he was coming?" asked the younger Hector.

"No, he likes to surprise me. Please just go! He'll be here any minute," replied young Carla as she shut the door on Hector.

"When are you going to tell him about us?" Hector cried at the closed door.

Hector shook his head and walked up the muddy lane.

"What the hell! Are you just messing with me? Didn't you say you knew Hector *before* we met?" Thomas asked Carla.

"This is the past. I'm not messing with you. I've carried this secret for years and hated myself because of it. I was seeing Hector before we met and we continued it again after." Carla said, loving the jealousy forming in Tomas' mind. A few more nudges and he would blame Hector for it all, she thought.

"You were cheating on me too?"

"Well, technically you were the affair I was having behind Hector's back. Then Hector started it up again after we were married."

"I knew it! I thought you were! I just couldn't be sure. Wait! So is Eve–"

Thomas saw something his mind couldn't quite cope with. A young man had appeared at the opposite end of the lane from where Hector had gone. He was heading straight towards them. The man was Thomas.
"What on Earth?" mumbled the present-day Thomas.
"Don't you remember this day? As I said, this is the past, try to remember."
Thomas from the past walked by them without batting an eyelid and walked into the house.
He tried to remember this day but it felt so long ago. He could recall the period around this time in his life quite well, but they were filled with a collection of days that were all quite similar. Days he would walk home from work and dread opening the front door. He used to argue with Carla a lot back then. All the arguments would usually be about stupid things, she just always seemed so angry with him for some reason. He also couldn't help but notice that Carla often looked flustered when he got home. He remembered back then that she had explained it away with reasons such as she had just finished the housework or some other physical chore.
Now it dawned on him, all the signs he had missed. He felt like such an idiot. Back then he had believed her without question. But now his stomach churned at the thought of Hector with Carla. To top it off he had no right to be angry at Hector. He was the one who had been cheated on first! With him no less! But if Hector

started the affair after he knew she was married, now that *was* something he could be angry about.

"All that time you were sleeping with him?"

"On and off, but yes. Sorr–"

"Don't keep saying it! You weren't then and you aren't now!"

"But Thomas—"

"Did he know about me?"

"He knew I was married, but he didn't know who you were. I don't think he even cared what your name was."

"How long?"

"We met when we were kids, but then didn't see each other for years. It was about a couple of years before we met, I met him one day in Lana—"

"Did you ever stop seeing him before you left?"

"Yes, I stopped it as soon as I found out about Eve."

"And Eve might not even be mine?"

"I don't know." She lied.

"You what!"

"So that's why you left? You didn't love me and you didn't want to come clean about Eve?"

"I was young. I didn't know what I wanted and I tried getting everything Tom."

"Do you still love Hector?"

"Hector? No. It was purely physical between us, he was such a good–."

"I don't want to hear it! Of all the things, I never thought you would do that. Then again I never even dreamt that you could take a child and tell me she was dead!"

"I just wanted the best for her, Tom. I thought in the city she would have a better chance. I mean, ok, I was young and greedy, but I always had her interests at heart."

"Why didn't you tell me? We could have worked something out! She was my daughter too! When I thought she'd died I— I . . . How could you do that to me? To her?"

Carla fell silent. Thomas sank to the floor and sat with his back against a tree trunk.

"I can't believe this. So much to take in. Was I really that blind?"

"I'm sorry I took her Tom, I really am. I was stupid all those years ago. When I found out she might have special powers and I could have them too, I think I went off the rails."

Thomas felt exasperated by such an understatement. "You think?" Then it dawned on him, who he was dealing with and what she had done in the past. "How do I know all this is true? How do I know you haven't made it all up?"

"To be honest, you don't. But, would I say this if it was a lie: Ask Hector yourself if you don't believe me."

Breakout

The whole tower shook violently, ceiling panels fell down, lights crashed to the floor leaving exposed wires dangling. On the laboratory floor the lights had gone out completely.

Pockets of smoke loitered in the corridors as various wires hung precariously from the broken ceiling sparking violently. They crackled and sparked in that special way that only seems to happen on movie sets after such a calamity. It seemed like the building contractors had just slung a few high voltage cables in the ceiling, loosely connected them and gone home.

Yorik and Grace stepped over the rubble that was the remnants of their room. Alarms blared as they scurried down the corridor and headed towards the lifts. Yorik slid to a stop in front of the well polished doors and Yorik pressed the call button. It blinked and flickered with a dim red outline.

"Shouldn't we just take the stairs?" Grace yelled above the deafening alarms.

"Carla's office has no public stairwell access, security and all that. The only way in is using this, or the service elevator. Who knows how many floors are above us? You fancy a climb before meeting our nemesis?"

Grace tried to block out the noise and focused her mind, trying to locate Carla. She soon found her, a hundred and seventy-two floors above them. She felt the bright pinpricks of light in her head of Thomas and Hector.

"A hundred and seventy-two floors, to be precise."

"I don't know about you but I don't fancy that many stairs."

"Our forms never get tired Grace, what's the problem?"

"It's just, the thought of them makes me tired."

Grace stared at Yorik as if he was more like a giant cabbage than a squirrel. She slapped her paw to her face.

"What about Hector and Thomas? They're still on this floor!"

"Have they escaped? Should we wait for them here?" asked Yorik.

Three large stocky guards careened around the corner and stepped in front of them. They drew their sidearms and took aim at the two squirrels. The lift pinged and the doors opened.

"Don't move!" the guards barked.

Yorik looked at Grace, Grace shrugged in response to the unspoken question. Yorik clicked and the guards fell to the floor.

"I don't think they are yet. They're on this floor I think," Grace said, completely unfazed and returning to Yorik's questions.

They turned away from the lift and walked up the disheveled corridor. They came to a small open area that led to several rooms. A blue protective shield

shimmered across the entrance to each of the wards. In the one directly in front of them they could see Hector and Thomas, they were yelling at each other. Thomas held Hector by the throat.
"How do we get past this thing?" asked Grace as she tapped the shield and it crackled.
"We wait."
"Wait? Does your master plan say for how long?"
"Not long, look, it's happening already," Yorik said, pointing at the blue shield. The barrier started to flicker. It grew in brightness then flickered again.
"What's happening to them?"
"It's losing phase-sync. The building's power lines have been ripped apart and it's struggling to maintain a steady backup power supply to the fields. They need a steady stream to maintain phase alignment. With us blowing up the floor I imagine the transformers are on the brink of burning out. The whole system should overload shortly."
Sure enough, the flickering became more frequent. The periods between it flickering back on grew and grew till eventually, it went off and stayed that way. The floor was plunged into an eerie light as only the emergency lighting remained on.
"What the hell?" asked Hector, rubbing his throat as he stepped from the room.
Thomas followed him out, looking equally as confused. They caught sight of Yorik and Grace.
"Was this you?" Thomas asked.

"Kind of," said Yorik.

"In a round-about way. But you are truly valued in this escape and your contribution was vital to our escape," Grace said, winking at Yorik.

"Where's Carla?" barked Thomas.

"Upstairs, a hundred and seventy-two floors."

"I need Carla to get to Eve. And YOU!" he said pointing at Hector. "Can bugger off! Just count yourself lucky your head is still attached to your body."

"I still don't understand what the hell you are on about? I told you I never realised she was your—"

"All those times I came home and you'd been with her! Carla showed me!" he said through clenched teeth.

"Bury it till we deal with Carla. It's been a long day and Thomas, you need to cool down. Hector, imagine how you'd feel if you just learned your wife had an affair with the man you've just met."

Thomas growled at Hector whilst Hector shrunk back a few steps.

They walked back in deathly silence to the lift and stepped over the still unconscious guards. Yorik pressed the call button again. The lift pinged instantly and the doors slid open.

"How come the lifts still work then?" asked Grace.

"Different circuits with multiple redundancies," answered Hector. "The lifts are the main exit so they have to work."

They entered the lift and Grace tapped in the floor number on the touch screen and the door started to close.

"More of your work by any chance?" Hector asked the squirrels, pointing to the unconscious guards.

Yorik shrugged.

The lift accelerated quickly upwards.

"So Grace, did you find out what Carla's up to?" Yorik asked.

"She's trying to set Hector and Thomas against each other," answered Grace.

Thomas glared through the side of the giant squirrel's head. Hector shrunk further into the corner.

The lift pinged its arrival at the top floor. The doors slid open and they were face-to-face with Carla's receptionist. He looked startled as the two large squirrels pounced out of the lift.

"What the hell?" he yelled as he dived under the desk.

"Er, hi," replied Grace.

"Hi," said Yorik as he sauntered up to the desk and leaned against it.

This really didn't help the receptionist. He didn't quite know what he expected from giant squirrels but he certainly wasn't expecting them to talk. He reached up over the desk to press the button for the intercom to the inner offices. Yorik saw the move and made a gesture with his paw. A bolt of bright blue shot out and hit the receptionist's hand. He jolted his hand back under the desk then seconds later they heard the thump as his body fell to the floor, completely immobilised.

"Nice, subtle," said Grace.

"Damn right, if I wasn't trying to be subtle half the wall would be missing."

The squirrels bounded into the room beyond. It opened out into a large waiting room with no windows. In the far corner by the only other door there was a smart looking desk with another prim receptionist sat behind it.

"Excuse me! What are you doing here? Terry never said–"

She didn't have a chance to complete her sentence. Yorik fired another spark of blue from his paw and she slumped forward onto her desk. Yorik and Grace hardly missed a step and continued to run towards the door, Hector and Thomas in tow. Yorik reached the door first and with his paw outstretched to push it open. He slapped into it. The door had failed to open. Iit hadn't even budged. Grace skidded to a halt behind him, barely stopping.

"Locked eh?" said Grace as she helped Yorik back to his feet.

"What gave it away?" Yorik replied, rubbing his forehead.

Carla

Behind the door, Carla shifted uncomfortably in her once luxurious executive leather chair. It now had a serious lean to it. Most of the rubble had been cleared away and a temporary desk had been found. A very unsturdy looking affair that propped itself against the ground.

She felt the presence of the squirrels and assumed the thump at the door was them. She breathed in deep, and slowly exhaled letting the anxiety flow from her. Carla sat back in the chair and waved her arm at the door and it magically opened.

"Thomas, Hector, come in."

They trundled through the doors and shuffled towards her wonky looking desk sat amidst various rubble piles.

"Yorik, Grace. Thank you for ruining my laboratories by the way."

"Well, if you insist on kidnapping and imprisoning people," replied Yorik.

"And what exactly were you doing in Preparation Station Theta?"

"We were concerned our friends here had been wrongly abducted."

"Yorik, this isn't our battle, it's theirs," said Grace.

"You're right, sorry Thomas."

Everyone turned to Thomas, expecting him to launch a tirade upon her. Yet as he stood there, he seemed

broken, a shell of himself. His eyes held a sadness that only grieving parents could even begin to comprehend.
"Where is she Carla? I need to see her again. It's been so–" A tear flowed down his cheek as his voice broke.
"Well I told you I don't know exactly where she is, but I can tell you where she might be. I'm sorry Tom . . ."
"Aren't you a councilor? Can't you find out?" he asked.
"I'm a counselor, yes, but a lowly one. I have access to the Caverns for meetings, but I couldn't get anyone else in and I certainly can't find her. I don't have the clearance."
"Brilliant, so just tell us how to get to the Caverns then?," snapped Yorik.

"But I don't know where it is. I just get taken there when they need me."
"Could you give us a vague area at least?" asked Grace.
"No, they take us there in air transports that have blacked out windows. I haven't the faintest idea where it is," lied Carla.
"So how are we supposed to find it then?" asked Thomas.
"Wish I could help," shrugged Carla.
"Hang on, why can't you just go in there and get her out? As you're her mother?" asked Hector.
"Because Eve has teams of people watching her and monitoring her movements. I don't think you get how

important she is to the council, to the whole world even."

"What?" said Thomas.

"Those powers she has, they're natural! Do you get how amazing that is? How unique? Her abilities have the potential to save us all."

"Save us? From what?" asked Thomas.

"The Bactamrin."

"The what?" asked Thomas.

"Bactamrin, the alien race that's imprisoned our planet."

"Alien race! What the hell are you talking about?" cried Thomas.

"Do you remember the place we found you in?" soothed Yorik.

"They were under mind control the whole time. They won't remember anything about it." said Grace.

"We were what?" asked Thomas.

"You were under mind control, but if you try, you will remember. Those memories are still there," said Yorik.

"I remember a drone. I think it fired on us?" said Hector.

"But what has this to do with Bactamrin? And our planet?" asked Thomas.

"Bactamrin," corrected Grace, "The place we rescued you from—"

"Rescued? My guards incapacitated you and brought you here!" scoffed Carla.

"That might be what you think happened, but how sure about it can you be? Didn't you think the weapons were a little conveniently effective against us? Considering you don't even know who, let alone what, we are?" said Grace.

Carla reached her hand under the corner of her desk and appeared to press something that seemed taped to the bottom of the desk, it wobbled worryingly as she did. Grace watched her, bemused by her, then she continued.

"The point is, the place you were being held. It was a temporary holding facility for humans. It is where humans are held until they are ready. They then get shipped off to the Bactamrin's orbiting ships for consumption."

"Consumption?" Thomas and Hector chorused.

"Yes, your species is being harvested, by the Bactamrin. The Council is making a very handsome profit from it all too."

"What!" cried Thomas, he turned and focused his rage on Carla.

Carla saw the look in his eye and quickly jumped into his mind. She channeled all the anger that was directed at her into his rage towards Hector. Carla skilfully guided the raw coursing waves of emotion directly onto the painful, swollen lump that Hector represented in his mind.

Thomas's face boiled with rage. He stopped mid stride towards Carla and turned on Hector. He raised his arms as if to push Hector away from him but, instead of making contact he stopped short. A low thud filled the air and a shockwave flew from his hands directly towards Hector. It hit him in the chest and he was propelled off his feet and backwards against the wall.

"What the hell was that?" Hector said picking himself up, his back and arms were sore and bruised.

"I dunno, it just—" Thomas mumbled, confusion filling his face, but his rage returned.

Hector saw Thomas raise his arms again and shielded himself against the onslaught. His mind flooded with fear and panic. Thomas yelped in pain and crumpled to the ground.

"What on Earth?" said Hector, dropping his guard. He noticed the squirrels were also holding their heads and looked like they were in pain. Yorik punched Hector in the leg.

"Ow!" said Hector.

The pain in everyone's heads subsided.

Thomas clambered back onto his feet. He made another shoving motion with his hands and Hector was pinned back against the wall, hovering a couple of feet from the floor. Thomas looked completely bewildered but also happy with the result. Hector tried to mentally kick out at Thomas again. Nothing happened. The waves of emotions that flooded out of Hector overwhelmed Thomas. He wavered and Hector slid down the wall.

Thomas fought back against the mental onslaught but with such confusing feelings coursing through him, he was losing ground. Hector was pushing Thomas into unconsciousness. He felt angry, sad, joyful, miserable, caring, and hatred all at the same time. Thomas tried to run from the violent buffeting of memories that flashed through his mind. But he was retreating from his senses and the real world. He was losing consciousness.

As the darkness engulfed him, he saw a well of shining white light, a pure power emanated from it. He felt it was his being, his will. He dived into it and the power flowed over him, then through him. As it seeped into his body, he felt it charging every cell. There was a sense of electricity flowing through him. It started in his toes and surged through his limbs. As it hit his chest it exploded out of him, projecting outwards from his head and hands.

He raised his palms towards Hector and let it flow. The air quivered in front of him. Everything was thrown back and away from Thomas. The tempered glass windows of Carla's office shattered and blew outwards. The wall Hector was pinned against collapsed under the pressure of the wave. Sparks arced from his hands to the sides of the room, crackling as they discharged.

The confusion in his head stopped and he lowered his arms. His anger, no longer fuelled by the manipulations of Carla, subsided. When the dust and debris settled, Thomas looked at the destruction around him. He heard Carla moan from somewhere under her desk. The desk itself had been shunted across the room and was resting against the wall. He could neither see nor hear Hector. Half the wall had been blown backwards into the next room. Any traces of his anger evaporated into concern for his new found friend. Sure, finding out their affair had hurt him, but he never wanted to physically hurt him. He thought about it, but didn't want to really.

"Hector?" he called.

Carla groaned.

"Hector?" Thomas called again, slightly louder this time.

There was no answer. Thomas scrambled over the remnants of the wall and over the rubble on the other side. In the darkened room he found Hector's body, half buried beneath chunks of wall. Thomas freed his body and pulled him away out of the debris. He checked for signs of life and luckily, Hector was still breathing.

"I'm ok, thanks for asking," Carla said, peering through the wall.

"This should be you!" Thomas spat.

Grace hopped through the wall, dust clinging to her fur. They could hear Yorik cursing in the next room as he climbed from the upturned furniture and other detritus. Grace sought out Yorik's mind.

Are you alright Yorik?

Yeah, my leg hurts, or whatever the hell these squirrel leg things are called, Yorik replied. Grace could feel his pain and grumpiness.
Do you need any help?
No, I can fix it, just give me a second. Help those idiots in there and watch that manipulative witch.
I tried to stop her from leaping into his mind, but she's surprisingly skilled at it.
Grace peered through the hole at Carla.
"Can't you restore some light in here or something useful?" Grace barked.
"Fine. Here." Carla clicked her fingers and a small orb of bright white light appeared in the middle of the two rooms, where a wall used to be.
"Grace! Can you help Hector?" Thomas asked.
"I imagine so," she said, shaking the dust from her fur. She hopped over the wreckage in the room to Hector's body. Grace took a quick look over Hector's body and held her paw over his forehead. Thomas thought he could make out a small glowing light emanating from her paw.
The air in the room vibrated. Hector's eyes opened.
"Hector," said Grace calmly.
Hector murmured in response.
"Is he going to be ok?" asked Thomas, his face full of concern.
"Yes, I think so. He's a little bruised, but mostly ok."
Unbeknownst to the group, Carla was slowly inching towards the gaping hole where the windows had once been.

"Hey! Where do you think you're going!" cried Grace at Carla. Carla turned and leapt through the window hole.

They rushed to the opening and saw Carla plummeting down the many stories below them. Then, about twenty floors down, she vanished.

As the group stared hopelessly down, guards piled into the room from both ends. In a few moments the room was filled with the noise of priming laser rifles as their heads were also being targeted.

The Caverns

The air throbbed from the pulsing of antigravity engines as the transport landed a short distance in front of Carla. She climbed aboard the ship via a door that slid open the moment it touched down. Carla tapped the destination she wanted into the touchscreen panel just behind the empty cockpit.//
It was the Caverns.//
The autonomous machine rose gracefully into the air and sped off towards the range of hills that rose in the West. Carla tried to use the ship's communications system to contact The Council but there was no reply. She contacted her assistant back in the tower.//
"Jake?"//
"Yes ma'am, are you ok?"//
"Fine, fine, I ended up in a field just east of the main complex. Where are they?"//
"They're under armed guard in your office."//
"Good. Can you contact The Council? I can't reach them."//
"No ma'am, the Caverns have been unreachable for an hour. Support is working on it. They seem to think it's the Tower's broken systems disrupting the network."//
"Hmm."//
"What do you want me to do?"//
"Keep trying to reach The Council. If you get through, tell them to lock the place down and wait till I get there."

"Yes ma'am, and what should we do with the prisoners?"

"Lock them up in the remaining detention cells if you can, but I imagine they'll be escaping soon."

"Escaping?"

"Seeing as our shielded labs couldn't contain them, I don't think our guards will hold them for long. Why do you think I'm heading to the Caverns rather than returning?"

"Shouldn't we do something then? Will the Caverns be safe?"

"Just hold them for as long as you can. Give me time to reach the Caverns and prepare. The Caverns should be safe enough; the elder psychics should be able to stop them."

"Yes ma'am. And ma'am?"

"Yes Jake?"

"Forgive me for being so bold, but what should I do?"

"Stay out of their way and they won't harm you. They are only interested in Eve. If they leave the Tower, head to the Caverns as soon as you can."

"Yes ma'am."

She closed the call and opened the control panel to the navigation computer. She tapped override on the speed limiter and the transport lurched forward with a fresh burst of speed.

Deep inside the palatial Caverns of the Councillors, Eve was being shown to her room. Technically she guessed it would be called a cave, but the opulence of the room she entered made the word cave sound ridiculous. The room was large and spacious with a high ceiling. Several unseen light sources lit the room in pools of calming colours. It made the room seem enchanted. There were sofas, chairs, and small tables placed thoughtfully throughout. The main sitting room led to separate areas which she presumed led to bedrooms and bathrooms.

The only thing the room lacked was windows and natural light. Eve was amazed by the beauty, the finery of every exquisitely handcrafted piece of furniture and its carefully planned placement.

The guide left her and she busied herself exploring. She was peering into a large, finely decorated bedroom when she heard a strange but pleasant noise. It artificially echoed through all of the rooms. Eve headed back to the main room and padded across the soft thick carpet to the door. A peculiar green light was pulsing over it and the sound chimed again, this time much louder and directly in front of her. She realised it must be the doorbell. She opened the door to a smartly dressed man, holding a tray of drinks.

"A pleasure to meet you Miss, my name is Rupert. I have been asked to extend to you any hospitality you may desire. Simply press the yellow button on any of the panels around the apartment and I will be here as soon as I am able. Please, take a drink."

"Thanks."

"My pleasure Miss." He bowed then turned to leave.
"Wait!"
"Miss?"
"Please don't call me Miss, my name is Eve."
"That would not be appropriate, Miss."
"But didn't you say I can ask you for anything?"
"Not quite Miss, but as you wish, may I suggest a compromise of Miss Eve?"
"Better, I guess. It's nice to meet you Rupert."
"The pleasure is mine. Anything else Miss Eve?"
"Is there anyone else like me here?"
"Sorry, Miss Eve?"
"There are a lot of older people, like my mum, but I haven't seen any children yet."
"The Caverns are reserved for the Councillors and their direct families. There are younger people here, but they are in the family quarters. They are deeper down in the Caverns."
"So how come I'm not down there?"
"You are an honoured guest Miss Eve, that is why you are in this suite."
"Honoured guest? But why?"
"I'm afraid it's not my place to say Miss Eve."
"Oh."
Rupert saw the tortured look on her face, a look that was lost somewhere between confusion and loneliness.
"However, Miss Eve, if I were to hazard a guess, I would imagine it is because Councillor Carla is a very

high-ranking member of the Council. That and maybe they need you for something very important."

This made Eve smile, but it was quickly replaced by more confusion.

"I'm sorry, but that is the limit of my knowledge Miss Eve. If I may, could I be excused? There are still a lot of preparations for the Councillor's arrival to be made."

"Of course! Sorry. Thank you, Rupert."

"My pleasure, Miss Eve."

Rupert left the room and the door closed with a solid thump. Eve waited a few moments for Rupert to be clear of her doorway then she tried to open it. The door refused to move.

Trapped again, she thought. It was no different than when she was living at the tower. She had everything she wanted, yet the outside was forbidden to her. A prisoner. Here was no different.

She wandered over to a large luxurious sofa and flopped onto it. A holographic panel was projected into the space in front of her and instantly images appeared on it. It highlighted the many options of entertainment available. One of the panes was reporting the news from around the world, she pointed at it and the image enlarged to fill the whole panel. Sound erupted from unseen speakers, seemingly all around her. The reporter was yelling over the sound of explosions and crowds rioting.

Eve's thoughts wandered back to memories of her dad. They were very dim and distant, more glimpses of another life than anything concrete. She could remember his face, his bright blue eyes that seemed to glow with a light of their own. His warm beaming smile that instantly made you feel safe, protected and loved.

Then there was a section of her memory that was filled with dark times. It seemed like every day her parents were shouting at each other. She couldn't quite remember much after that, but that was when her father had vanished. It was around then that they had moved to the tower. A lot of her memories started to merge into her present life with her mum after that. She vaguely remembered the time her mum had brought her to the city but then never took her home again. She pleaded with her mum to take her home and cried non-stop when she didn't.

Carla explained to Eve that her father had left them and that her home was now the Tower. For ages she refused to believe it, she simply didn't want to. She couldn't believe the father she loved could do that to her. Then, one day, Carla had given in to her requests and taken her back home. They found their old house empty, deserted. It had been left empty for quite a while.

Back in Burnim, Eve had been given everything she had wanted. Although they never let her out into the rest of the city. She was always visiting the roof garden. It was the only fresh air she had access to. When she asked her mum why she wasn't allowed out,

Carla would claim that the city was too dangerous for her. Eve didn't dare complain, she was living in a cage. Eve fiddled with a panel she found on the side of the sofa, trying to turn the screen off, till eventually in frustration she cried.
"Turn OFF!"
The hologram switched off and the room was plunged into a deafening silence. Eve turned her attention to a bowl of fruit sitting on the table in front of her. She focused on the apple on the very top of the pile. Eve guided it into the air and the apple rose upwards. She made it hover in front of her and started it spinning slowly.

Squirrels?

With a loud pop, Hector, Thomas, Grace, and Yorik appeared in a patch of dense woodland. Thomas was standing in a patch of boggy ground. Each step was met with an unpleasant squelch. The smell was horrendous.

"What the hell?" cried Thomas.

"Well if you insist on fighting." answered Grace.

"I didn't fight it. It just scared the crap out of me! What was that?"

"Teleporting."

"What?"

"Teleporting, we bend spacetime to redirect matter to wherever, or whenever, we want," answered Yorik.

"What?" Thomas asked again.

"We can move around instantly to wherever we want. Within reason," explained Grace.

"Within reason?" asked Hector.

"Yeah, there are certain boundaries we cannot cross. There are 'Rifts' in space time that we can't teleport across. So, we can't, for example, teleport to certain distant star systems."

"Oh, why's that then?" asked Hector.

"We don't know for sure. We just know that things get distorted across those rifts."

"What do you mean star systems'?" asked Thomas.

"We're not actually here," replied Carla to a very puzzled Thomas. "Yorik and I are projections from a spaceship that is heading towards Earth. But there's several rifts between us, and the distance is immense, otherwise we'd teleport straight here."

"It's limited by distance then?" asked Hector.

"Not really, it's just limited by our ability to channel the energy needed for greater distances. The greater the bend, the more energy you need to do it."

"So where *are* we then?" interrupted Thomas.

"We're roughly where Carla teleported to," answered Grace.

"Roughly?"

"You have to be close to get an accurate trace on who you're following. Carla had already fallen quite a way by the time she teleported."

"So, where do we go now? Do we even have a plan?"

"The caverns are that way," said Yorik, pointing towards the nearest of rock faces that imposed from the left and front.

"Carla's close, somewhere over there," Grace said, pointing in the opposite direction from the cliff.

"She's not even at the Caverns yet?" said Thomas.

"It's protected from teleportation. She's having to fly the remaining way," replied Yorik.

"How do you know about all this and that alien nonsense Carla was spouting?" asked Hector suspiciously.

"It's not really nonsense, it's really happening," said Grace.

"We're actually from a galaxy you astronomers never found. A very long way from here but from a planet not unlike this one," added Yorik.

"What!" cried Hector and Thomas in unison.

"We're not the same as the Bactamrin!" Grace quickly added.

"You're aliens?"

"The talking squirrel thing didn't raise your suspicions?" toyed Yorik.

"So why are you here? Why are *they* here?" asked Thomas.

"We're here to save you. Well, here to help you save yourselves at least. We defeated the Bactamrin attack on our planet at great cost to our species. We couldn't let them devastate another, so we followed them across our galaxy."

"But how come they are harvesting us then? If they're still heading towards us?"

"They sent out search parties to comb the universe for life they could feed on. One found yours and they must have established a base in your system. They duplicate at a phenomenal rate. The main body of them turned and fled the day we conquered them. We've been tracking them ever since and their course is currently heading for Earth."

"Where are the Bactamrin from?" asked Hector.

"All we know about them is that they are some kind of Cliatia species. They tried—"

"Sorry, What's Cliasheea?" asked Thomas.

"It's our word for, uh, the closest would be insect, I think."

"So, you're aliens then?" asked Thomas again.

"Not to us, to us you're the aliens," said Yorik smiling.

"And squirrel is your natural form?"

"No, our form is something quite different. We project our minds into these creatures and without knowing this world, we had to assume creatures of an average level," answered Grace.

"So why squirrels?"

"This is where you end up asking questions that spawn more questions."

"But I can't help but ask–"

"I know, I know, but if we can get through all of this without your species being wiped out, we will answer all the questions you like."

"Alright."

The deep throbbing of pulse engines broke into the conversation, a sleek black ship zipped through the air above them and headed straight towards the cliff.

"That was her," said Grace.

Hector and Thomas stood staring blankly as they processed all the information they had just been given. Yorik and Grace hopped away towards the cliff. Hector watched the giant squirrels bound away through the foliage and thought to himself that, even by his standards, the past forty-eight hours had been pretty weird.

Lock the Cavern Doors!

Carla's transport circled the landing pad on top of the highest hill of the Caverns. Away to the south she could just make out the valley of Lana and the lake that stretched to Halmington.

Carla smiled at the thought that Thomas and Hector had almost walked by the entrance to the Caverns on their way to the preparation station.

Looking at the valley she almost envied the blissful ignorance of the common people. To live in a quiet village where life seemed to be such a peaceful existence to her life now. For the common person there were no aliens, no complicated political games to play. Even the disappearance of their aging populace was made out to be some benevolent retirement plan.

Unless you were one of the selected of course, they had a different journey altogether.

The ship eased itself gently onto the landing pad. It had barely touched down when Carla jumped out and ran towards the roof access door. She burst through it and barged into her assistant, Rupert.

"Rupert! Get this place under lockdown NOW!"

"Ma'am?"

"DO IT!"

Rupert saw the panic in her eyes and ran inside to the nearest control panel. With Carla at his heel he tapped in the emergency code. Alarms rang out across the complex. A solid metal shutter slid over the door to the

landing pad, when it locked into position the control panel glowed with an eerie red light, then turned green as the other doors to the Caverns were locked down.
"What's wrong, councilor?"
"The squirrels, I think they're on their way here."
"Squirrels?"
"You know The Squirrels."
"Oh."
"Indeed. I need you to gather the Council, we need an emergency meeting on act Fifty Four, right now."
"Ma'am." Rupert turned to leave.
"Oh, and where is Eve?"
"Suite Delta, two five."
"Good, good. Let me know when the Council is assembled, I'll be with Eve."
"Ma'am, don't you wish to freshen up? Your apartment is ready too. I can arrange for Eve to meet you in the lobby?"
"No Rupert, I shouldn't leave her alone right now. If the squirrels somehow manage to break in, I need to be with her. I think Eve may be interfering with our communications too."
"Yes Ma'am," Rupert said, then turned and left hastily. Carla followed Rupert along the corridor for a while then took the first turn on the left, towards the lifts. She hurried up to them and pressed the call button. It felt like an eternity waiting for one of them to arrive. Once inside it was an even longer wait as she descended the floors to Eve's suite. The lift pinged its arrival at the

floor, the doors had barely started to open and Carla was squeezing through the gap. She sprinted down the corridor and slid to a stop outside Eve's door and pressed the bell, a few seconds passed and Eve opened it.

"I thought we were going to meet—"

"Are you alone?"

"Err, well yeah. Who else would be in here?" Eve said, confusion clouding her face.

"Hopefully no-one, but we have a security alert. Rebels might be trying to get into the Caverns."

"Rebels?"

"There has been an uprising, some of the peasants have found out the location of the Caverns and could be heading this way as we speak. Can I come in?"

"Yeah, do I have a choice?" Eve swung the door wide open behind her as she stomped off towards the sitting area. Carla joined her on one of the large luxurious sofas.

"What are peasants? And why are they rebelling?" Eve asked.

"It's what we call the people who can't see the world that we live in."

"Why can't they see it?"

"We shelter them from it. They wouldn't be able to handle seeing the real world we live in."

"So why are they rebelling if you're protecting them?"

"It's complicated. They think we shouldn't protect them from it, that it's their right to see the world as it is."

"What's wrong with that? Seems wrong to be lying to them."

"But they're stupid! The only reason they think they want to know the truth is because they don't know what it is. If they did know they would only wish they didn't know. We are shouldering that burden for them, but they're too ignorant to appreciate it."

"Sounds a bit like you enjoy controlling them."

"We might control their lives in some ways, but it's for their own good."

"Own good? How do you know what's best for them though?"

"Because we are wiser than they are, they wouldn't understand."

"That sounds a little—" Eve was interrupted by the door chime. Carla walked over and opened it to reveal the tired looking face of Rupert.

"Ma'am, the council is assembling now."

"Great, thank you Rupert."

"Ma'am, forgive me for being forward but several of the members were less than happy about the last-minute meeting."

"I can only imagine how some of those grumpy old gits might have taken it. Thank you, Rupert."

"Ma'am." Rupert was taken aback by the direct appreciation. He bowed awkwardly then turned and walked off down the corridor. Carla closed the door to face a quizzical looking Eve.

"Do you remember what I said about the Council?"

"Yeah, they're the people like you who look after the country."

"That's right, and remember that trick I taught you?"

"The one where I see what's in people's heads?"

"That's it. And you remember how to alter their thoughts?"

"Yes."

"Now, I'm going to need you to use that trick on a few of the councilors in this meeting."

Attack of the Squirrel!

Yorik, Grace, Thomas and Hector reached the edge of the woods and stood looking at the rocky cliff dominating the sky in front of them.
"How are you doing, Thomas?" asked Hector.
"I still can't quite believe Eve might be alive!"
Grace looked at Thomas. Like watching the weather unfold on a stormy day, she could feel his emotions criss-crossing. She saw the pain in his eyes. The joy in his smile. The anger in his fists. His poor heart exploding with emotion in the middle. In the rush to stop Carla she hadn't given a thought to what Thomas might have been going through. As Yorik said, empathy was not her strong point.
"We'll get her back soon," she said, then put her furry paw on his arm and patted it. "We'll save her."
Thomas looked down at the squirrel. Its face contorted into something he guessed was concern. But in her straining state, it looked more like she needed a shit. Broken from his revere he scowled. But quickly he melted into a smile of gratitude, for the effort it seemed to be involving if nothing else.
"For so many years I thought she was dead. I just can't believe it. How much time have we lost? How many first time moments have I lost? How much of her life have I missed?"
"I think she'll understand it wasn't your fault. As for the time you've lost with her, well, why fret over

something you can never get back? It's better to focus on the years ahead that you will have with Eve. Let's just get her back first."

"So how do we plan on getting in then?" asked Hector.

"I think that's the back gate over there by that large fissure," said Yorik pointing towards the cliff in front of them. Hector followed his finger to a dark mark that looked like a scratch down the side of the rocky face.

"Right then, let's go."

"Hang on, Thomas," said Grace restraining him. "We need to get past the guards. If we're lucky Carla won't have raised the alarm yet, but even if she hasn't, there'll still be security to get through."

"I'll check it out," cried Yorik as he scampered off along the edge of the forest.

"Yorik wait!" cried Grace, but he was already out of earshot.

"He's eager," said Hector.

"It's because he's an empath. He feels the emotions of others and sometimes they course through him with such ferocity it's hard for him to separate other people's emotions from his own."

"You mean he feels what we feel?" asked Thomas, guilt clouding his face.

"Yeah, and I'm afraid it is mainly you, Thomas. But he won't hold it against you. Who wouldn't be feeling emotional in your situation?"

"I wouldn't quite say I was feeling emotional."

"Who wouldn't be feeling a storm of raw emotions in your situation?"

Thomas's eyes began to tear up, he swallowed hard and turned away.

"Shouldn't we follow him?" Hector asked, breaking the uncomfortable silence.

"I guess we should," Grace replied. Watching the turmoil of the poor Thomas, she actually felt sorry for him. A feeling she was quite unused to.

They followed Yoriks tracks along the edge of the forest, sticking to the cover of bushes and trees. As they neared the fissure, Yoriks track veered from the treeline and headed straight towards it. Only a few shrubs and smaller trees broke the otherwise clear ground between the forest and the cliff face.

In the darkness of the crack they could make out a large steel door. Outside it there were several guards armed with rifles. They all looked rather agitated and were pacing back and forth. Grace, Thomas, and Hector found a thicket to hide behind and peered out toward the entrance. Hector caught sight of Yorik. His furry shape was bounding towards the gate and the guards. In a blink of the eye Yoriks large form had split into several smaller squirrels. They all continued running towards the door. One of the guards noticed the scurry of squirrels heading towards them and alerted the other guards. They all stood staring in amazement at the numerous furballs now scampering headlong towards them. The miniature Yoriks were nearly on top of the guards when they raised their rifles and took aim. Just as they were about to fire, the squirrels leapt at the guards. The squirrels landed on their faces and clawed at their eyes. The guards cried in pain as the squirrels scratched and tore at their eyeballs. They tried to rip the squirrels from their faces but the claws sunk deep into their flesh.

Finally, the collection of Yoriks leapt down from the guards, leaving their victims blinded. The guards clasped blood-soaked hands over their empty eye sockets.

Each squirrel then appeared to melt into each other, increasing in size as they did. Eventually all that remained was the regular, albeit unnatural-sized Yorik. The guards stumbled around, fumbling along the rockface or floor. They were trying to work their way back inside the Caverns, however none of them really knew the direction they were facing. Four of them were heading away from the door and the other three were pawing at the ground trying to work out which direction they should head.

"It's clear!" cried Yorik.

The guards called out towards the source of the voice.

"Let's go," Grace said to Hector and Thomas.

They ran from their cover over the rough grass to the doorway, avoiding the stumbling guards and splatters of blood.

"Well, that was erm . . . graphic! Remind me to never piss you off," said Thomas.

"But how do we get through this?" asked Hector pointing at the solid metal door. There appeared to be no crack or visible division in it.

"Have you guys even tried to use your powers since Carla's lab?"

"Well yeah, but melting solid metal? I'm not even sure how it's supposed to open."

"Have you tried?"

"Well, no."

"Exactly! But alright, we'll sort this one, on the condition you had better start trying."

"Yeah, yeah, don't pretend you don't love saving our asses," chided Thomas.

Yorik stepped up to the door and held out his paw. He scrunched his face up in intense concentration. From the pad of his paw a burning bright red beam shot forth and hit the middle of the door. Where it hit the door the metal began to glow a dull orange. He kept projecting the beam for a full minute but nothing more seemed to happen to the door. Yorik refocused, shuffled a bit then tried even harder. The beam grew in size and intensity and glowed a deeper red. The patch in the door kept growing and turned a much brighter orange that bordered on yellow. Still the door remained solid. Grace, watching Yorik begin to struggle, stepped up and joined in. She also shot a similar beam of intense energy at the door but hers was a blinding electric blue. The whole door started to glow, passing from golden yellow to searing white. It started to shake violently as the squirrels focused. It seemed like the door would vibrate off its hinges or the rock face itself would collapse. Yet the door remained solid and would not open. A few rocks fell from higher up on the cliff, narrowly avoiding them. The heat from the door was so intense that they had to step back. Finally, the squirrels stopped, their fur matted with sweat.

"It's no good. It's magically protected," panted Yorik.

"Yep, Carla must have put the place on lockdown or something."

"Can't you do anything about that?"

"Be my guest Thomas, I need a laugh," said Yorik as he winked at Grace.

Thomas stepped up to the door, the metal had already returned to a dull orange and the heat was rapidly dissipating.

"So how do you do that beamy thing?"

Yorik slapped his head with his paw.

"Just imagine what you want to happen over and over, visualise it. Eventually it will happen," answered Grace.

Thomas tried to focus his mind. He imagined a beam of energy emanating from his palm and striking the door. At first, he felt nothing. He tried again and again, nothing. Eventually after several tries he felt a tingling sensation spread from the bottom of his spine all the way up to the base of his skull. Thomas felt the hairs on his body raise as a surge of energy grew from deep within him. It coursed through his body and made him feel like he could do anything. It was as if his whole body was coursing with power. It was waiting for him to direct it wherever he wanted. As he thought he might explode, he let the surge flow through his palm and towards the door. A fuzzy beam, a tenth as concentrated as the squirrels' attempts, shot from his palm and hit the door. The door started to glow again, but only a dull red. Thomas felt that the energy pulsing from his hand was draining something inside him, he had to stop. He rubbed his head as the sweat trickled down his brow, he felt exhausted.

"Screw this," he said, wiping his forehead again.

"Be careful of . . ."

Grace was interrupted as Thomas raised his hands to the door and imagined it exploding violently. He focused all his anger and injected into the growing energy inside him. The whole doorway started to crumble as the metal wobbled before them. Then it exploded.

The Council

Carla led Eve down a thick carpeted corridor to another set of lifts. These were more finely decorated and luxurious than those used to descend from the landing pad. She waved her hand in front of the platinum framed motion sensor.

"So, why do I need to make them vote against it?"
"It's complicated Eve, maybe you'll understand better when you're older."
"Don't say that! Just cause I ask questions doesn't mean I don't get it!"
"Ok, I take your point," soothed Carla, "but I think you might not understand it. The best way I can explain it is, remember when you were really young and the lightning storms would scare you?"
"Yeah."
"And you remember I'd tell you everything was going to be okay?"
"Yeah, I do." She smiled at the pleasant memory.
"Now you're old enough to understand electricity and weather, you understand what a lightning storm is?"
"Yeah."
"And so, you're not so scared of it now, because you understand it?"
"Well, kind of, I don't like the thunder."
Carla smiled, "Things like that are scary for different reasons as well, some never go away. But can you imagine how you would have felt if I'd explained all

about weather and electricity to you when you were really young?"
Eve thought for a while.
"I don't think I would have understood." she said.
"Exactly! This situation is a bit like that; if we told everyone what we know, the full facts and all the science behind it, people wouldn't understand. They'd be very frightened and panic. With you helping us we can direct their choices to benefit us all. It also keeps them all calm, and free to enjoy their lives."
"But that's different isn't it? Shouldn't adults know how to handle it better?"
"Not as much as you'd think Eve. Some adults are nothing more than scared children inside. It's our job to protect them from things that would terrify them and make their lives worse."
"But when will they get to find out about it?"
"Eventually they will, when they're ready. However, some may never be able to understand."
"But that seems unfair, can't they learn?"
"Maybe Eve, but—" The lift doors opened with barely a sound but it distracted them both enough for Carla to escape Eve's questions. Once inside the opulently decorated lift, they sat on the soft comfortable couch as the lift began to glide downwards.
"So, you know what I need you to do?"
"Yes but—"
"We're running out of time, Eve. We can talk about everything later if it will make you feel better. For now,

please just trust me, this vote cannot get through. It will undo everything we've worked so hard to build. Okay?"

"Okay. But can you answer just one question?"

"Okay, just one."

"If you don't want this vote to succeed, then why did you call for it?"

Carla was surprised by her insight. Eve was far too young to be asking such questions and it was quite unnerving.

"Well.... It's kinda complicated but the short version is that this vote was scheduled for a week from now. However, if I bring it forward and it gets defeated, it can't be voted on for another two years. That gives me time. Time to prove that the way we are following is the best."

"So why now and not in a week?"

"Those people I said that were on their way here, they might stop us by trying to do what I'm asking you to do, but to persuade them the other way."

The lift accelerated swiftly and smoothly, only the rapid increase in floor numbers on the digital display indicated just how fast they were now moving.

"How come the numbers are going up?" asked Eve.

"Eh? What do you mean?"

"The floor numbers. They're going up but we're going down?"

"Oh, they count ground level as zero, all the floors below that increase as you go further down."

"Shouldn't they have a minus sign in front of them?"
"I think it would be a bit silly to have a minus sign in front of all the floors, so they don't bother."
"Oh."
The elevator continued to drop, further and further into the bowels of the earth. Finally, they felt a gentle tug on their stomachs as it started to decelerate. The digits stopped increasing as they glided into alignment with the floor. The doors slid open with a whisper, revealing a grand lobby full of people talking excitedly. The walls were solid rock and they arched far above their heads. Elegant chairs and coffee tables decorated the large space. They walked towards the busy reception desk.
"Great, they haven't started to go in yet. Eve, we need to head up there, to the viewing gallery." Carla pointed at a staircase that climbed up the far wall.

They weaved through the busy crowd and climbed the stairs. At the top was an arched doorway leading to a large room. They walked through the arch and were at the top edge of a large cavern. The metal walkway they were on circled the entire room like a giant balcony made of scaffolding. The floor below them was carved into a large bowl and curved tables circled around the center at several layers. Under each layer of tables there was a glow that gently alternated between green, purple, and blue.

The room's only other entrance was a large doorway below them that led back into the lobby. The walls and ceiling were bare rock but illuminated by hidden lights that cast the ceiling in shades of colour that mimicked the sky outside.

At many points along the metal gantry there were pods that faced the center of the cavern. As they passed the pods Eve peered into them. She found that they were actually observation rooms filled with people. Most of them were full but finally they found an empty pod. Carla led Eve inside and activated an electronic lock on the door behind them. Eve sat down in the front row of seats and looked out on the expansive chamber. The pod had a glass front that started below her feet and stretched to the ceiling. Eve looked down and saw the floor of the cavern below her. It was a bit unnerving at first, being this high up, but Eve quickly adjusted and was enthralled by the activities below her. She noticed that most of the seats around the chamber were empty. However, there was a slow trickle of people coming in from the lobby. All of the people were dressed in long dark robes with hoods that shrouded their faces in shadow.

"Who are all these people?" asked Eve.

"Councilors. They represent all the different parts of the world."

"The whole world?"

"Mostly, some countries are still independent, but most of those are the smaller ones."

"Independent?"

"As in, they haven't agreed to join the global council, which this is."

"Why are some independent?"

"They think that joining the world council is bad and want to keep their independence by being outside of it. They feel better off managing their own affairs and acting alone."

"Oh, why?"

Carla sighed. "That's a good question Eve, but we don't have time for the explanation. Look! Can you see the group coming in now?"

The cavern was filling up quickly, at the entrance a large group of important looking figures had just entered. Eve guessed they were important since, unlike the others, their ceremonial robes were golden and their hoods were thrown back leaving their faces exposed.

"The ones with the golden robes?"

"That's them. They're the ones I want you to influence. They hold sway over most of the other votes."

"Who are they?"

"Some are powerful business owners. Others are the leaders of larger countries."

"But surely they know how they should vote already?"

"They should, but they have been persuaded to believe in things that are wrong."

"Like what?"

"Like, they have been led to believe collectively we have sufficient forces to fight back and stop the abductions. We don't. They have no idea what the aliens are capable of."

"But—"

"Eve I have to go. I called the vote so I need to get down there. Stay in here and wait for me ok? After everything is finished, I'll come and get you."

"Okay," Eve replied glumly.

"And you remember what I need you to do?"

"Yes," said Eve testily.

"And if they call for any amendments then listen to my thoughts ok?"

"Yes."

Carla rolled her eyes at Eve and left the pod. She ran around the gantry and bolted towards the stairwell and down to the lobby. Below Eve the group of golden robed Councilors had taken seats around the innermost ring of tables.

Eve sat patiently in the pod watching the final few people take their seats. She saw Carla hurtle into the room below. Her own golden robes she had hurriedly put on, were flapping behind her as she ran. About halfway to the center Carla stopped running and tried to regain composure. She had barely managed to calm her breath by the time she reached the center. Carla took a seat at the innermost circle.

Through hidden speakers in the pod, Eve could hear the general hubbub of the large crowd below her.

Eventually the noise began to die out and silence rippled across the room. A heavy weight of expectation and apprehension seemed to smother the atmosphere below. The golden robed figure next to Carla leaned in and nudged her. Carla stood up and made her way to a small raised circular platform in the center of the room. As she stood on it, a bright spotlight illuminated her from somewhere in the ceiling. She started to speak and her voice was amplified many times. The speakers in Eve's pod gave a small pop as they switched to Carla's microphone.

"Councilors. Thank you for convening at such short notice. As you all know this vote was scheduled for later this month, however, recent events have changed our situation. We need to come to a swift decision. We need to choose our path so we can take appropriate action as soon as possible."

Murmurs rippled through the audience. At that moment, almost on cue, a deep rumble resonated through the rocks around them and made the lights flicker.

"We are under attack!" Carla called out above the outbreak of commotion.

"By the Bactamrin?" a golden robed councilor yelled.

"No!"

"Who's attacking us then?"

"Squirrels!" cried Carla.

A Very Deep Back Passage

Thomas opened his eyes and tried to clear the vibrant swirling shapes that danced in his vision. He was lying on his back under what appeared to be a large piece of metal door. Thomas heaved the hunk of metal from him and slowly climbed to his feet. He looked to the cave entrance. Where the door used to be, there was now a large hole carved into the rock face. All that was left of the solid metal door were a few twisted shards, all that was left of the frame that had been embedded in the rock.

Thomas looked around for the others. Yorik was sitting back on his haunches a little way into the rough grass and Grace was walking back towards him. He couldn't see any sign of Hector and began to worry. Then he noticed another pile of rubble beginning to move a short distance from him. Thomas scrambled over the debris. He had barely taken two steps when the sky turned black. He fell face first into the rubble and passed out.

He drifted back to the conscious world and through the foggy haze he could hear voices.

"Is he alright?" Asked Hector.

"Yeah, he's just got a concussion I think. He passed out." Replied Grace

"Looks like he's coming around." Said Yorik.

"So how the hell did he blow up the door anyway?" asked Hector.

"Carla's experiment must have supercharged his abilities. His lack of control must have walloped the door with all his raw power. He's just bloody lucky it didn't backfire on him," said Grace.

"He's lucky to be alive." Said Yorik.

"Why didn't you two just blow it up then? Seeing as you have mastery of your powers." Asked Hector.

"You need to learn how to do this yourselves. The best way you can do that is by doing it." said Yorik.

"Hey, Thomas! Thomas! Are you ok?" interrupted Grace as she shook him.

Thomas opened his eyes slowly, even the glow from the deep blue sky sent stabs of pain into his brain. At the edge of his vision he could make out the faces of the two squirrels.

"Hey buddy?" said the upside-down face of Hector, appearing a few inches from his eyes. Thomas yelped. Hector helped Thomas to sit up. His head was throbbing and his stomach felt peculiar too.

"You okay?" asked Hector.

"I— ah, I think so." Replied Thomas.

"We know we should be asking you to take it easy, but we need to get moving. Can you walk?" asked Grace.

"I guess."

Hector helped Thomas to his feet. He wobbled slightly but soon regained his composure and seemed to grow in strength with each stride.

"Great! We should hurry, security will be all over this place." Said Yorik.

They headed towards the gaping hole in the rock and climbed over various pieces of rubble and debris. As they stepped over the remnants of the door they could hear alarms ringing in the distance. The corridor beyond the door was dark as the only lights dangled broken from the ceiling. At the end there was a plain-looking set of lift doors. Hanging precariously from the ceiling there was a sign pointing to the right. It had a symbol of a staircase on it.

"Should we take the lift?" asked Hector.

"No, they can trap us in there. Besides, who knows what Thomas's explosion has done to the wiring," answered Yorik, looking at the hanging lights and wires.

"It's more than two hundred floors down," cried Yorik. "Let's use the lift and stop a few floors from the bottom, we can get off there and take the last few flights of stairs."

"But won't they see us and stop the lift or something?" asked Hector.

"The explosion has hopefully wiped out the security monitors too," said Grace.

"Isn't that all the more reason for not taking it? As in, what else has it wiped out?"

"It'll be fine, trust me," said Grace.

Thomas pressed the lift call button. After a couple of minutes, it clattered and clanged its way up to their level. The doors opened with a worrying shudder and they shuffled inside. Grace typed 199 into the numeric pad and the lift started to hurtle downwards. The ride was rough and every so often there was a terrifying bang from the top. Eventually, the lift stopped plummeting and lurched to a gentle shuddering fall. It jumped and scraped into a rough alignment with the floor and the doors screeched open.

They left the lift and stepped into a long corridor carved into the solid rock. There were lights dotted all the way along it and several of them flickered. The tunnel headed straight towards the center of the mountain, seemingly forever. On their immediate left there was a worn red door. The door frame seemed to be fused into the bare rock.

They headed through it and out into an equally grungy stairwell. The metal staircase rose many, many flights above them. Below it dropped a couple of flights into what looked like water. They ran down the stairs and sploshed onto the flooded bottom floor. There were a couple of drains on the floor that were struggling with all the water that trickled down the staircase walls. An old wooden door was the only exit from the stairwell, after a few hard shoves it eventually opened. They followed the corridor beyond as it snaked back and forth through the solid rock. In places the ceiling dipped down so low they had to duck under it to pass. Eventually the tunnel widened and passages led off on either side that disappeared into darkness. The corridor finally came to an end at a set of metal double doors. Thomas and Hector barged them open and fell clumsily into the circular room. In the middle of the room was a large desk surrounded by a spiral staircase in the center of the room. The staircase descended through the floor. Around the outside of the room there were several doorways.

Seated behind the desk were three startled security guards. They stood up and aimed their pistols at the strange group of intruders.

"Freeze!" the leader cried.

"Wait! We're just trying to get to Carla," said Thomas.

"On the floor! Hands behind your backs!"

"Bugger this," said Yorik.

Yorik closed his eyes and focused his mind. The guards yelped in pain and fell to the floor, their hands clamped tightly over their ears.

"We need to get down that stairwell, Yorik said.

Thomas and Hector vaulted over the desk and started to descend the spiral staircase whilst Yorik and Grace hopped over the desk and clambered down behind them.

"Damn, it needs a passcode." Thomas called back to the squirrels who were now halfway down the stairs.

"Grace, check the guards, the one with golden bars, he looks like he was in charge," said Thomas.

"Hector, I think this is the perfect opportunity for you," said Grace.

"What? Why me?"

"Because your speciality is with the mind."

"But wouldn't it be easier —"

"You need to build up your skills, this is a perfect opportunity."
"But aren't we in a hurry?"
"Once you're in his mind, time will hardly pass by at all. Seconds become hours in the mental realm."
"Go on, don't doubt yourself so much. Besides, what's the worst that can happen?" added Yorik.

Hector climbed back up the stairs and sat in the chair nearest the decorated man. He tried to get comfortable, to calm his mind and focus his thoughts. However, with all the turmoil he'd just witnessed, he was struggling.

Relax Hector, you cannot direct your mind when your thoughts are out of control. Grace's calming voice echoed in his mind.

Easier said than done! How, in all this, am I supposed to stay calm?

Focus on just your breathing. Focus so that it is all that fills your mind, nothing else.

Hector took several deep breaths in and out, however random thoughts and worries overrode his concentration.

Those thoughts Hector, recognise them as the noise they are, then cast them away. Let your subconscious deal with those issues. All you have to worry about is breathing.

Hector let the distracting thoughts flow through him and he felt surprisingly calmer. But thoughts kept popping up. He tried again and again to let them flow through him. Eventually, like coming out of a storm and seeing the first few patches of clear blue sky. He slowly broke free of them.

Well done Hector, now, try to stop thinking about breathing and let your body take over that. Keep your mind empty and if the thoughts pop back in, let them pass.

Hector felt a panic rising at the thought of not focusing on deliberately breathing, as if his body wouldn't automatically take over if he wasn't thinking about it. The thought of suffocating brought back memories of his childhood. He realised the distraction as it raced around his mind and let it pass through him. He imagined what the deep blue sky would look like after a rainstorm and focused on that. Then his mind was clear and he was no longer worried about his breathing.

Good, very good. Now descend into your mind lake like I showed you.

He imagined being at the top of a flight of stairs. At the bottom the staircase opened up into a brightly lit swimming pool. Taking a step down with each long exhale, he was soon on the last step. There seemed to be no bottom to the pool in front of him. The water now up to his chin, was warm and comforting. He took a step forwards into the abyss.

Hector plummeted down through the waters of his conscious mind and was drawn through a swirling purple vortex at the bottom of his now dark mind lake. Hector traveled into the inner core of his mind. Everything before him swirled and resolved itself into new shapes. He was walking on a small globe that rotated through light and dark as he breathed in and out.

You're doing really well, Hector. I'm afraid it's getting hard for me to reach you now. Picture the person you want to connect with and a portal will appear to connect you to them. Once you're in there I won't be able to communicate with you. Remember where you are at all times! If you slip into believing what's in his mind is real, you'll never escape. To get home, just follow the tugging on your mind back to your body. If you ever start to lose the tugging feeling, head back immediately!

He pictured the guard's face and a swirling purple portal appeared. It was a tunnel that led through the collective consciousness of every living being. He plunged forward and felt the overwhelming power of the universal collective. The energy coursed through his soul and he felt an overwhelming sense of euphoria, a feeling that he was complete. Then Hector remembered his reason for being there and sought out the mind of the unconscious guard. He was guided to him and a tunnel instantly connected them.

Hector was plunged into the depths of the guard's mind. The man's memories swirled before him. He soared past moments from his childhood, through his training years as a guard, and then flashes of his dreams.

Hector searched the large vaults of the man's mind but he quickly realised it was futile, there were just too many memories. Hector floated up through the guards subconscious as if he were floating to the top of a deep lake. He neared the surface and prepared himself for the transition.

This was the trickiest part, or so Grace had told him, it could be confusingly chaotic. Grace had told him that entering someone's mind was hard and could lead to the transferral of emotions and memories. However, entering dreams and nightmares was a lot more dangerous. In those you could lose all sense of reality and become part of their mind. The thin tendrils that kept your essence connected to your body were stretched to the breaking point. If you lose yourself, anything could happen. The best scenario was that you took control of the host, the worst would be insanity. To be constantly disconnected from your own mind and body, believing that reality was someone else's nightmare.

Hector reached the surface and broke out into the man's current dreams. He was thrust into the middle of a delirious vision, the manifestations of the man's dreams.

The sky above him was dark and stormy. Lightening flicked across the dark stormy sky, before him lay a large empty plain. A gust of wind blew, tripping across the ground it left a wake of small vortices. One of them rose up and toward him, stinging his eyes. On the ground in front of him a pile of crumbled clothing rose into human form, it was the guard.

"Who are you?" the guard asked.

"I'm here to help you. What's your name?" replied Hector.

"Peter," he replied with a vacant look in his eyes. "Where has it gone?"

"Where has what gone?"

"The Myriad, it nearly got me this time!"

"The Myriad? What's that?"

The landscape morphed before his eyes. The deserted plains bent and shot skywards to create massive snow-capped mountain ranges. They stretched upwards around them. Once the ground had stopped morphing, they were on a plateau between two tall peaks. The thunderstorm rolled into a heavy blizzard that blinded the rest of the scenery from them.

"Oh no! It's coming, it's coming!" cried Peter. He started to climb and run blindly up the mountainside.

"Wait!"

Hector had a brief moment of clarity, he held onto the fact he was in Peter's dream. This was where he could so easily lose his grip on reality. He thought back to the training Grace had given him and he slowly began to gain control of the dream world. He changed the mountains and blizzard into an image of the control room. Peter now sat at his station by the spiral staircase. He redirected Peter's fear of being chased by the Myriad into believing it was behind one of the chamber doors. He put the suggestion into his mind that his only option to escape was the spiral staircase.

"Peter, it's coming." prompted Hector.

Peter sprang to his feet.

"You're right, I can feel it. We need to leave." He started to run towards the stairs, then he stopped. Some memory seemed to come back to him and he turned towards one of the doors.

"No! There's another coming from that way too," cried Hector as he planted another menacing presence behind the door he faced.

"Arrgh! We're trapped!" Peter yelled.

"What about the stairs?"

"Yes! It's our only hope." Peter bolted down the stairs. He ran like death was chomping at his heels. Hector raced after him, barely reaching Peter as he started to enter the code. Hector watched him carefully as he tapped in the six-digit code. In the elation of his plan succeeding, he let his projection of the world slip. Everything morphed again. The control room was now a dark cave with no cracks or windows. He had no idea where they were. A small flickering flame in the distance cast a dim and eerie light around the cave. Hector realised the floor was moving but he had no idea why. Peter stood next to him, rigid with fear.

"What on earth is wrong with the floor?" asked Hector.

"It's . . . it. . . . it . . ."

"It's like there's a load of–."

"Insects!"

"Yeah, oh."

Hector felt several things crawling up his legs.

"RUN!" cried Peter.

They sprinted towards the flame and leapt into its protective aura. A terrifying growl echoed from somewhere deeper in the cave behind them. They peered into the mirk trying to see its source. At the very edge of the meager pool of light that the flickering flame cast, they could just make out the glint from two very large eyes. The eyes started to approach them. The light revealed a glinting set of razor-sharp teeth. There seemed to be flesh hanging from its mouth. The menacing eyes drew closer and closer, then stopped. It stood, panting and breathing heavily, just shy of the light, hiding its full form. They felt a small reassuring comfort in the flame as it appeared to be holding the monster back. The beast let out a bloodcurdling roar. The flame flickered. Then it went out.

The Proposition

"What do you mean Squirrels? I thought the Bactamrin were more like insects than squirrels?"
"They are, Councillor Jensen, but these are different aliens. They are here to break up our agreement with the Bactamrin," answered Carla.
"Who and what are they then?" asked another councilor.
"Where are they? Do we need to evacuate?" another councilor from the front bench asked.
"Evacuate because of a squirrel attack?" mocked Jensen.
"They aren't just squirrels! We believe they are another species of alien from a quite different part of the universe than the Bactamrin. We suspect that they are actually projections of their consciousness onto squirrel hosts. We don't know why they're here or what they want. The only thing we do know is that they seem to be trying to disrupt our relationship with the Bactamrin. It's why we need to vote on our next phase of integration with the Bactamrin, we need their protection."
"At what price?" cried a voice from the back of the chamber.
"I don't think this is the right time for a vote, Councillor. If we are under attack, we need to secure the Caverns first."

Carla looked up pleadingly at the capsule where Eve sat watching the proceedings. Eve knew what she wanted, although it went against the gut feeling she had, she did it anyway. She focused on the energy shapes of ones that held the largest sway and with a surprising ease she steered their ego laden thoughts to agree with Carla.

"No, we must vote," said Jensen.

"I agree, let's use this chance while we are all here. Then we can deal with security," agreed the lead councilor. "Carla, state your proposal for the vote."

Carla smiled and glanced up at Eve's pod.

"Thank you, Councillor. Everyone here must feel that our arrangement with the Bactamrin is far from perfect. But the question I ask you all now is, isn't any arrangement of peace better than an all-out war? A war that we have no way of winning. We are technologically inferior. We are outnumbered by at least a thousand to one and we have been surrounded by their warships for the past two decades. If we hadn't entered into our agreement with them, the human race would be extinct right now.

"That is why we need to maintain our agreement with them, no matter the cost. It far outweighs the destruction they would cause if we declared war with them. The horrible truth is that we need to work with them.

"Which brings me to the issue of the sacrifices and the secrets we keep from the common people. Some of you believe that we should not be keeping the real-world a secret from the poorer uneducated folk beyond our privacy shields."

"For those of you who think like that I ask you this: would the lives of the villagers, the farmers, and everyday people really be any better if they knew the truth? Would they have happier lives living with the fear of the Bactamrin orbiting our planet? Would they sleep easy in their beds knowing the Bactamrin regularly takes people because our flesh is regarded as a delicacy to their palates? Would the panic created by such news not lead to the wasteful loss of life and a complete breakdown of our society?"

"But why should our people live and die like peasants when we have the technology to improve their lives?" shouted a different voice from the back of the room.

"A fair point and somewhat true. Their lives could be improved, but they would also face the complications and stresses of living in a technological age. Few of us here are old enough to remember the times before we built the privacy shields and hid our advanced cities behind them. The time before our technology and knowledge was restricted to the more select populace. Well back then our highways were permanently clogged with traffic, the city streets were filled with the homeless. Everywhere you went there was overcrowding and fighting over limited resources. Utility companies couldn't keep up with the demand being placed on them from the burgeoning populace.

The very air we breathed turned to poison from the pollution of an overwhelmed system stretched to breaking point.

The system we have now works, there can be no denying it. Who here can really look inside themselves and not feel that warm glow of being privileged? We are all in an exclusive club, a VIP lounge if you will, and deservedly so. Whom of you out there, if you are really honest with yourselves, don't relish that feeling? Do you really want to lose all this and become average people again? To fight with the rest of the commoners against the Bactamrin?

"My proposal is simple: we move forwards with the Bactamrin agreement to the next phase."

A confused applause rippled awkwardly around the assembly as they all seemed to wrestle with their feelings. Carla walked from the spotlight back to her seat and slowly the applause grew throughout the crowd. Carla wondered how much of that was her speech and how much was Eve's influence.

A slender cloaked figure stood up from the bench directly opposite Carla in the inner circle. She walked gracefully over to the spotlight and began to speak in a soft gentle voice that seemed laced with a hidden power.

"Councilors. An intriguing argument from Carla, I'll agree. Full of haunting half-truths and loaded with fear. You see, behind the fear of war, the complications of our own egos, and the threat of what our future would be like if we had no agreement, lies a very simple issue. It's a moral issue. A simple case of right or wrong with nothing in between.

"Is it right to sacrifice our own people? Is it right to let an invasive species harvest our own kind? Is it right to sacrifice vast swathes of our own kind so we might live? Shouldn't we be fighting for these people? Aren't we all here to make decisions that will protect everybody? Don't we have a moral obligation to fight for the existence of our own species? Is our self-importance and ego stroking really worth the loss of life?

"If you think ego is more important than life, perhaps we deserve to be hunted to extinction! We cannot let—"

The lady staggered backwards and clapped a hand to her forehead; her face crinkled in pain. Several councilors rushed to help. Carla looked up at Eve's pod and smiled again.

Up in the pod, Eve was struggling with the speaker's mind. The others had been relatively simple to control but she was much stronger. Eve strained to keep a grip on the ladies' thoughts and she was slowly losing control. Finally, Eve let out a yelp and was thrown out of the speaker's mind.

The speaker regained her composure and freed herself from the supporting arms around her. She walked back to the spotlight and glared at the shocked face of Carla.

"Sorry, it appears we might be more compromised than we realise. If I could ask the guardians to increase the interference fields please?" She waved to the guards by the doorway, they nodded in return.

"Carla mentioned the old days, when resources were tight and privileges were few. Back then we had two choices: to restrict technology and split our society or to learn how to grow up, to be a better species. We needed to evolve our way of thinking and our behaviour. Instead of making things more precious by restricting them, we need to help people lose the desire for them. The only way to do this is to learn how to eradicate greed. However, that means we all need to take a giant step forward in mental evolution. We need to stop defining ourselves and judging our self-worth by comparing material value against our fellow humans. That is the hardest part. It's also the most crucial.

"We can only ever learn to share our resources, our technology, our possessions, if we learn to value them for what they are, or are not as the case may be. If we can't let go of this, we will always find a way back to the place we are in now.

"But that is why we now have a unique opportunity. We can start again. We can educate and begin to build the world we all deserve to be in. A home where we no longer turn a blind eye to the atrocities the aliens inflict upon us. A world where we can all live in safety. A home where we are all happy and content. A world where we have the united strength to defeat any attack the aliens might throw at us. But best of all, we would do it as a free species, a species that pays tribute to no one, a species that stands up for whatever part of our planet you might be from. This is our Earth, our birth right! It's time to take it back!"

Applause rippled throughout the assembly, there were even several overexcited cheers. Then the clapping died away rather unnaturally. Eve was hard at work on their minds. The guardians were making the job a lot harder but compared to the mind of the lady speaker, it was relatively easy.

Control

Hector closed his eyes, not that it achieved much as it was already pitch-black. He was desperately trying to block out the sounds of everything around him. The rustling of a million terrifying creatures crawling over the ground towards him. The slow heavy footfall of the giant beast as it stalked them. Peter started to whimper then he broke into a tormented wail.

Hector sought out the internal tunnel back to his own body. Through the dark depths of Peter's tormented dreams and thoughts he found no trace of the purple tunnel back home. The sound of the creature seemed barely an arm's length away. He felt like he was losing touch with his own reality. He tried to change the scenery.

Instantly the dark cave vanished and they were back in the control room. The room was empty apart from Hector and Peter. Hector had no time to imagine all the details. It was then he heard the voice. The familiar voice of Grace.

"Hector, you're still in his mind, escape it like you would your own."

"Grace?"

"Who's Grace?" asked Peter.

"You can't hear that?"

"Hear what?"

"Of course!"

"What the hell are you talking about?"

Grace was right, he knew what he had to do. He couldn't believe he hadn't realised before now, but he was adamant he needed the purple vortex to get back home. He had forgotten to descend back into the depths of Peter's subconscious mind before he could reach the portal.

He closed his eyes and imagined he was on a desert island surrounded by calm blue waters. Hector stood on the beach facing the ocean, the warm water lapped gently over his feet. He took a step into the water and stepped down as if he were descending a staircase. The water rose halfway up his shins. Hector took another step and the water rose again. Each step into the water it got deeper and deeper, till at the ninth step, the water was just below his chin. This was back to the tricky part. He took another step forward. The water rose over his face and above his head. His first instinct was to hold his breath but he needed to keep breathing, to relax, but he couldn't. He eventually calmed himself and remembered that in this realm he didn't need to breathe. Against all instinct, Hector opened his mouth and the water filled his lungs. He was waiting to drown, yet he felt no discomfort, no sudden panic. He felt very calm as he began to sink deeper and deeper into the water, the sandy floor beneath his feet dropped away. He sank far into the darkness and the light around him failed.

Soon the light from the surface vanished completely but he was still falling into the murky waters. Hector started to worry. He was sure he should have reached the bottom by now. He felt his non-existent heart race in his mentally projected chest.

Then the bottom appeared out of the gloom. Directly below him there was a vortex spiraling through the sandy floor. He took an imaginary deep breath and fell through it.

Beyond the vortex he found himself in Peter's subconscious; standing on the rotating world of light and dark. He was at the mercy of Peter's mind again, the light and dark sections passed by beyond his control. He noticed the passage of them was uneven. The dark, evil side lasted much longer than the brief skip through the light, pleasant side. In his dark side the creatures from the nightmares ran free and untamed. He felt like he was on a terrifying roller coaster that kept dunking him into Peter's terror. He desperately searched for the purple vortex that led out of his mind. After many cycles he eventually caught sight of it in the evil depths of the dark side. He lunged for it and fell into the incandescent tunnels inside.

Hector quickly found the way back to his own mind and opened his eyes. He instantly regretted it. The bright lights of the control room dazzled him, leaving a glowing after-image in his eyes.

"Are you okay, Hector?" asked Thomas.

"Mmm, m'okay. The code is 459037. Go and get the hatch open. I'll be alright."

Thomas ran down the spiral stairs and tapped the combination into the pad. A green light appeared above the panel and the hatch blocking the stairs slid back, revealing the room below. At the bottom was a small room with a solid metal door. The room was lit by a solitary red lamp somewhere in the ceiling. The light gave the room an eerie feeling. Yorik and Grace climbed down after him and sat on the last step of the spiral staircase.

By the door there was another panel, this one had no numeric keypad, it had a lens covered hole in it.

"What's this?" asked Thomas.

"A retina scanner I think," answered Yorik.

"What?"

"It scans your eyeball and uses the image to verify it is the right person," Grace explained.

"How the hell are we going to get through that?"

"Well, if only we had someone with the skills to take on the exact physical appearance of one of the guards down there?" Yorik said, rolling his eyes.

"What? Me?"

"You're the one who has the shapeshifting abilities! We took you to see Gaia for just such moments as this!"

"If you're not really squirrels then you have the ability too," Thomas fired back.

"Ours isn't quite the same. We don't shape shift; we project into these forms. Besides, you need practice."

"Alright, but if all hell breaks loose, you're sorting it."

"Seeing as you blew the back door in, I think our ninja-like approach has probably been noticed."

Thomas huffed and climbed up the stairs to take another look at the guard.

"I think he should be the one to deal with them out there too," Yorik whispered to Grace, seeing the guard's energy shaped through the solid rock walls.

"Maybe, be careful how much we push him though," she replied.

Thomas scanned the face of the guard and tried to keep the image in his head. As he climbed back down the staircase, he focused on all the features he could remember and his face slowly morphed into that of the guard's.

"Hey, you're getting the hang of that!" exclaimed Grace as Thomas appeared behind them.

Thomas leaned his head towards the scanner and peered into the eye scanner. He was blinded by a red flash and then it went dark. There was a small pause followed by a beep and the red light above the door turned green.

"Well, that was easy!" said Thomas as the features of the guard faded from his face and he returned to being Thomas.

"I'm afraid the hard part is about to start," said Yorik.

"There're guards outside the door," added Grace.

"Probably a lot of them," said Yorik,

"Right okay, so how are you going to handle them then?"

"We're not," answered Yorik.

"What the hell are you doing here if you're not going to help us?"

"We are helping you. Do you really think that if we save you every five minutes it would actually help you?"

"Well, kind of—"

"All jumping into help does is make you rely on us. Then you will need us, depend on us, and consequently, never learn how to look after yourselves. We might not be around forever. We might need to help other species. This is about your species standing up for itself. I suggest you start that by learning to use the abilities we worked hard to get you!"

"Hard to get? You asked Gaia to give them to me!"

"You think that was the first time we spoke to Gaia? No. We have been trying to persuade her for the last ten years to get involved and help her precious species."

"Really?"

"Yes. Believe it or not we have been working hard to get to the point we are now in. Use your powers Thomas, develop them."

"How can I do that then? Morphing I did by accident and learned to control, but attacking soldiers? I wouldn't know where to begin."

"Thomas, you blew open a solid steel door. Whatever you need is in you, find it, then flow with it."

Thomas started to panic. He knew the squirrel was right; but when he had used his powers to blow up the door, he had nearly killed them all. Now he had to deal with a room full of guards! But then an idea popped up from that magical place of intuition. He pictured the next room and somehow, he could sense all the people in the small room. He focused his mind on an empty space in the middle of the room. Thomas projected an intense ray of invisible energy right into that space. The air started to vibrate. As Thomas focused more and more energy into it, the vibrations increased. Inside the room he could sense the guards becoming uncomfortable; they could hear a low-pitched vibration that was increasing in volume. The volume increased until one by one, the guards collapsed on the floor.
"Well, I'm impressed.," said Grace. She had been watching the events in her own mind.
"That certainly was quite something," added Yorik.
"I'm not quite sure how I thought of it, or even how I did it."
"That's the power of your subconscious, it's quite surprising what we actually know how to do, but our conscious minds convince us we don't."
"It doesn't seem to affect you much though?"
"We evolved past such physical boundaries long ago."
"Evolved? So, your species is much older than ours?"
"Much, much older. Anyway, more guards will be coming soon. We should move," said Yorik.
Hector joined them at the bottom of the stairs.

"Why are we hanging around here?" Hector asked.

"Exactly," cried Yorik.

Thomas pushed the door open and led the way into the room. It was quite a small room with no windows and only one other door. The rest of the room was taken up with monitors displaying camera feeds from the many rooms around the Caverns. Several unconscious bodies were laid on the floor.

Grace stepped over them and pushed open the next door, having felt no human presence behind it. The room was a long and narrow corridor that ran from left to right. The wall they faced was completely transparent and looked out onto a circular assembly chamber. The cavernous room was full of robed figures and in the center of the room a bunch of gold-robed figures stood arguing. Carla was one of them.

"Hey that's Carla! But what on earth is going on in there?" asked Thomas.

"It's the councilors meeting chamber, this gathering is probably the work of Carla."

"She's in there? I can't see her!" said Hector peering through the transparent wall.

"Yeah, there!" said Yorik, pointing at the center of the room.

"Where's Eve?" asked Thomas. "Grace, can you sense her?"

"I can't, too many minds are out there."

"There," Yorik said, pointing up at a pod suspended from the top of the ceiling. "Hector, Tom, go and get

Eve. Grace, I think it's time we had a little chat with Carla."

"I agree."

"But how are we supposed to get in there? The corridor looks like it goes on forever," Hector asked, peering down the corridor as it arced around the council chamber.

"Thomas?" Yorik prompted.

Confrontation

The head Councillor stood in the spotlight and addressed the assembly.

"Councilors, you have heard the arguments for and against the passing of Act 54. Please cast your vote accordingly. The voting period will end in fifteen minutes."

There was a rumbling of movement and chatter throughout the council as they slowly cast their votes on the terminals in front of them. As more and more of them completed their votes the chatter rose in volume and excitement.

BOOM!

The back of the room exploded in a shower of glass and debris. Before any shards hit anyone, they froze in mid-air. The shrapnel floated motionless above the heads of the assembly. The terrified screams and shouts died out, replaced instead by the chatter of confusion and awe.

"Nice touch, Yorik," said Grace as she hopped down from the now exposed corridor in the rear wall.

"Yeah, it's a pretty cool effect isn't it," gloated Yorik. "Although Thomas, you are getting much more controlled with your demolition skills. Very impressive."

"SQUIRRELS!" yelled someone from the crowd. The whole room erupted in panic and started stampeding away from Yorik and Grace.

"STOP!" boomed Yorik. The whole room froze.

Yorik moved his paws about and the floating debris moved towards the doorway. The shards coalesced into a pearlescent barrier that stretched out to cover it.

Hector and Thomas climbed down over broken lumps of wall to join the squirrels.

"You two, get up there and talk to Eve, she's already trying to get into our heads," said Grace.

"But how? The doorway has been—"

Yorik clicked his claws and they were transported instantly up to the metal platform circling the room.

"—blocked."

"FIND HER!" yelled Grace from the floor below.

They ran around to the nearest pod.

On the floor below, fear of the unknown creatures had immobilised the Councillors. They had no idea what the squirrels were.

Carla broke the silence.

"Leave Eve alone! Why are you attacking us? What do you want?"

"We don't want anything from you! We're certainly not attacking you. We're here to help."

"Help! You break in, damage our defenses, rip a hole in our Council chambers, and you claim you're here to help?"

"We're not here to help you, we're here to help them," said Yorik, sweeping his arm over the crowd.

"What? I'm here right now, fighting to save us all!"

"No, you're not! You're fighting to keep things the same! You're afraid of what change would mean and the power you'd lose! You're killing your fellow humans because you want a privileged life? How sick is that?"

"But you would rather see all of us killed in a pointless war!"

"We're not the ones making a profit from the blood of our own species," spat Grace.

Carla's face contorted in a mixture of rage and panic. She held her hands out in front of her and touched her fingers together, forming a triangle. A ball of fire formed in the middle of it. She made the fire grow until it filled the gap between her fingers and then flung it towards Yorik. Yorik stopped the fireball mid-flight. He blew towards it as if blowing out candles on a birthday cake and the ball of flame spluttered out, leaving nothing but a wisp of smoke.

Carla cast an intense blue beam of light from her palms. Yorik raised his paw in response and as the light hit his paw it was absorbed without effect. He closed his eyes, showing nothing but a mild twinge of pain. After a couple of seconds, the beam slowly began to fade. Yorik opened his eyes and the blue beam flicked instantly to an intense white and appeared to flow back towards Carla. Carla screamed in pain. She let her arms drop to her sides and the beam hit her in the chest. She was catapulted back across the room.

Yorik stopped the beam and Carla climbed to her feet, rubbing her chest. She looked around the room, all the councilors were looking at her, waiting for a reaction. Most of the faces appeared to be filled with hatred and mistrust, but there were a few sympathetic ones too. But she could tell Eve was losing the battle with them. She figured one of the squirrels must be blocking Eve's mental manipulations. She realised then she had lost. Carla clicked her fingers and vanished in a swirl of dust.

"Damn! I thought you sealed the room Yorik!"

"I have! That was on top of the existing seals on this room. She must have a secret channel out of here."

On the gantry above the Councillors, Thomas and Hector had found Eve.

"Eve?" asked Thomas, hardly believing his eyes. It was his little girl; he could see it in her eyes but she was so much older. She was a teenager.

"What do you want with me?" Eve said. They felt a sudden pressure on their minds, as if they were several stories below water. Thinking was like trying to stir syrup.

"I'm . . . your . . ."

"Oh my god," she gasped. Eve had read Thomas's thoughts. The pressure on their minds fell away.

"Eve, I can't believe . . ."

"Dad," she cried and ran to him. He opened his arms and they hugged.

"I thought you were dead," she mumbled into his chest.

"Carla told me you were dead," he said, stroking her head.

"Are you okay though? Are you hurt?" Thomas said, breaking the hug and looking closely at her.

"I'm fine. I never thought I'd see you again."

"I can't believe you're really alive!"

"What about mum? Where has she gone?"

"It's complicated, she . . ."

"You really hate her? Don't you?"

"What?"

"I can read it in your thoughts."

"That's a little unnerving Eve. But yeah, you're right. After what she's done to us, I do hate her."

"Sorry, your thoughts are quite loud. What are those squirrels doing here?"

"They're actually here to help, so they say. Do you know where Carla might have gone? Does she have a safe place?"

"I'm not sure. She always left me in the tower. She might have gone back there I guess. But Dad, you're only going to talk to her right?"

Thomas sighed.

"I don't know Eve. Apart from the hideous lies and what she's done to both of us, she has caused so many innocent people so much pain. Then took some of their lives too."

"I know Dad, but it's mom."

"Have you seen the things she's done?"

"No, she won't let me into her mind. But I have seen the human holding stations."

"So, you know we need to stop her?"

"Well, yeah. But I don't want to lose her either! I only just got you back!"

"I get it Eve, we'll try our hardest to persuade her to stop. Anyway, I don't think we'll find her back in the tower, it's too obvious."

"We should get out of here," said Hector. "The squirrels down there might need our help."

"I don't think they need anyone's help," replied Eve. "Who are they?"

"I think the question is more, *what* are they?"

"They seem to be helping us so far. They aren't from Earth, that much we know. They say they are aliens that project their minds into the squirrels' bodies," said Thomas.

"Different aliens? Or the same ones?"

"Different. But it's a long story, Eve. Let's talk about it after we get out of here," Thomas said.

"We need to get down there. It looks like they're getting over the shock of seeing the squirrels." said Hector.

They left the pod with Eve clutching Thomas's hand. They made their way around the steel gantry to the exit and ran down the stairs into the deserted lobby. As they clicked along the marble floor they could see the sheen of the reconstructed glass force field covering the entrance to the Council chambers. They skidded to a stop a few paces from it. Peering through they wondered what the shimmering layer might do to them. Could they pass through it?

Hector reached out first, extending his hand towards it. His fingers touched and the hairs on his arm stood up. His arm tingled with pulses of energy. Hector pushed his whole hand forward and felt the warm air of the assembly room beyond. He took a step forward and passed through to the other side. Thomas and Eve jumped through after him.

"And why should we listen to you?" the golden-robed council member asked Yorik.

Yorik saw the three of them arrive through the shielded doorway, seemingly unnoticed.

The room was filled with chatter.

"Quiet!" boomed Grace.

The council members grumbled and murmured to an unsettled silence.

"We are here to help you. Fight them or not, we will still battle them. But we also want your species to survive. We want you to fight the Bactamrin, in fact, we want to help you build what you need to do that. We are a species, much the same as yours, but our home is very far away." she paused to let them absorb. "Thousands of years ago we were attacked by the Bactamrin. Back then we were less developed and technically inferior to the Bactamrin, much as you are now. We barely survived, but we did and we want to help you do the same."

"Why?" asked a voice from the crowd.

"Some of our leaders made agreements with them not unlike the one Carla made for you. For centuries our species suffered, we were their fodder; to be eaten whenever they wished. Eventually though, we advanced our technology in secret and fought back. Eventually they tired of their losses and left our system. Then, several years ago we received a message from your planet.

"What was the message?" asked the nearest golden robe.

"The message was a cry for help, many, many years old. We figured it was purely an accident that the transmission was picked up as far away as it was. Nevertheless, we heard it. We recognised your assailants as the same species that attacked us. We felt that we could help, that we should help. No species should suffer the near annihilation we did."

"So, if you're from another planet, what the hell were you doing hiding in the forest?" Thomas called out from the doorway.

"Thomas! We haven't been hiding, we were waiting. Waiting for the right circumstances."

"Whilst our people die?" called out another voice from the crowd.

"Yes, sadly we couldn't help you right away. You weren't ready to fight back," Grace said addressing the source. "Only now have you reached the point where you feel that you might be able to fight them. Imagine what you would have done if we had come to you before now?"

"But how can we believe any of this? How can we trust you?" said Eve.

"In truth, there is no way of knowing for sure. You just have to learn to trust us. However, I can give you this assurance: If you want our help we are here, if not, then we'll leave, peacefully."

"How can you help us against the Bactamrin?"

"We can help you build shields and defenses that will keep them out of your atmosphere."

"Forever?"

"For a long time, long enough for our fleet to reach here and support you."

A gasp rippled through the whole audience.

"Relax! We are not invading," she said irritably. "If you don't want our help then we will leave these bodies, return to our ships, and continue to fight the Bactamrin. When they have been eradicated, we will return to our home."

Yorik saw the look of confusion in the Councillors' faces.

"These squirrel bodies are just a projection of our consciousness. We aren't really here. We are on a ship traveling towards this planet. We have borrowed these forms from your world's wildlife and temporarily inhabited them. It's the only way we can be here in order to help you prepare in time, whilst our physical bodies are in transit."

"How long till your ships arrive?"

"Ahem, one hundred and fifty-two years."

The council chamber broke into more rumblings and chatter.

"So how can two squirrels help us against the Bactamrin for one hundred and fifty odd years?"

"Don't underestimate them! You have seen only a fraction of what they can do," piped up Hector still standing by the translucent shield.

"Indeed, there are more than two of us. Several hundred of us are working around this planet. They are waiting for the right time to help."

"What! Several hundred of you?"

"We aren't interested in taking your planet from you. We will leave if you want us to. We are here to help teach you what you need to survive."

"Why? What's in it for you?"

"I can understand you asking this question, but for us, the question isn't why do we want to help. The question is why wouldn't we want to help you? The only way your species can evolve is to move past your own desires and needs. Not everyone or everything is out for its own interests. We want to help because we have lived through our own invasion. Our own catastrophe. We know how it feels to lose millions of souls. We want to help you because we can."

"And what about Carla?" asked Thomas.

"Carla has made some bad decisions, she thought she was protecting your species but unfortunately, she was misled. You and Hector will track her down and bring her back here for you to give out whatever justice is deemed fitting," replied Grace.

"What are you going to do now?" asked the lead councilor.

"Nothing. Absolutely nothing. I suggest you re-cast your votes now you know the full picture. Then, if you want the Bactamrin gone, you can vote on whether you want our help or not. We will wait outside."

Frozen Where The Heart Is

Yorik and Grace led them out of the archway, dropping the shield as they passed.Outside, the Council ironically shut the great doors behind them and the chamber sprung into life like an angry beehive.

"So, we're going after Carla then?" asked Hector.

"Well, you two are, we're staying here for the outcome of the vote," answered Grace.

"Wait! What about Eve?"

"If you wish to leave her in our care, we guarantee her safety. But you might be surprised to find she doesn't need protection."

"But . . ." Thomas looked down at Eve. After all the lies he had been led to believe for so long were shattered, he couldn't bear the thought of leaving her again so soon. It was as if leaving her would make the dream fade and he'd never see her again.

"Dad! It's ok, if you trust these squirrels then I do. I want to help fix this mess, and say sorry."

"What have you done?" Thomas asked gently.

"She made me turn the councilors minds to vote the way she wanted, agree with her and stuff. I knew it was wrong but I just–"

Thomas knelt down to look Eve directly in the eyes. His bright blue sparkling from the artificial lights.

"Eve, it's not making mistakes we should be sorry about."

"What?"

"We should be sorry if we don't learn from the mistake. Every time we find we have done something wrong, we get the choice. Do we learn, or do we continue hoping others won't happen?"
"What can I learn from influencing people to keep us from sacrificing people?"
"Why did you do it?"
"Mum did, she made it seem so sensible."
"You said you felt it was wrong earlier?"
"Yeah, it just felt, something here, above my belly. I wasn't happy."
"That could have been your intuition."
"So you mean I should listen to that?"
"If it feels natural, like you're flowing down a stream, it's usually right."
"I still feel I can do more here than I can catching her."
"Okay, I just—"
"It's okay dad. Go get her. Bring her back alive, please."
"Of course."
Thomas hugged Eve, it was a connection they had missed for too many years.
"So how do you reckon they'll vote?" Hector asked Yorik, breaking the emotionally charged silence.
"I don't know. Hopefully they will see we are just trying to help." Replied Yorik.
"I think they are still cautious of us, the unknown, but I think they are seriously considering letting us help them," said Grace.

"I still don't get it," said Eve. "Why would Mum make me change their minds and agree to more people being killed?"

"I think originally she wanted to stop the slaughter from the random raids on your people. Now, I think she has too much vested interest in the Bactamrin. With the connection she has with them, she holds great power by proxy. I think she is finding it rather addictive." answered Yorik.

"I don't feel it's the wealth though," said Grace. The others turned to face her. "She's terrified of what would happen if you don't give them the tributes. She has been convinced by them that they are far superior, and are in a greater number than they currently have."

"This is just paranoia then?" asked Hector.

"Wouldn't you be in her position? She's been dealing with the Bactamrin for years, striking deals she didn't want to make. Listening to their boasts and gloating about wiping other worlds and species out. She knows they want to do the same to Earth," replied Grace.

"You're saying we should feel sorry for her?" asked Thomas.

"It never hurts to try to understand people and what is driving them. Empathise with them. But she must be stopped.," said Grace.

"So how do we find her?" asked Thomas.

"Grace, can you locate her?" asked Yorik.

"Yes,"

"I'll transport you both straight to her," said Yorik.

Then clicked his claws.

Thomas and Hector vanished from the lobby and were flung across space time to pop back into the living room of Thomas's old house by the lake.
"Hey, isn't this—"
"—my old home, yes," finished Thomas.
They looked out the back window and saw Carla sitting on the end of the jetty. She was dangling her feet in the water.
The backdoor was open and they walked out onto the wooden platform.
"So, you found me. What took you so long?" said Carla, still staring at the water.
"I can't believe I didn't think of this place myself. I should have known. For all your power seeking, betrayal, and kidnapping, your heart still beats. This is where we started our family."
"Can you remember the first time Eve swam in this lake? I remember it like it was yesterday. This house is full of memories."
"If you miss our family so much, why the hell did you destroy it?"
Carla looked up and stared at Thomas, the forstiness behind her eyes returned, it made him shiver.
"It's simple Tom, I really don't value our family. I love our daughter. The memories I have of her growing up are some of the most treasured moments in my life. But

that's where the family ends. I have no feelings for you, Tom."

"Did you ever have feelings for me?"

"Once, I think. But then it all got so complicated. Somewhere it left me feeling numb. Not just to you, but to everything. Then there seemed nothing holding me back from doing whatever I wanted. So, I did."

"You always fancied him?"

"Hector? Please! He was a distraction."

"Were there others?"

"There were. But they were even less interesting than Hector. I took Eve and ran when I could. I got a better offer in the city and took it. It seemed so simple, so easy, because I could do it all without feeling anything."

"But you took my daughter!"

"I thought about breaking up, but it would have been too messy and dragged things out. Besides, it was more convenient to make it seem like Eve had disappeared."

"That's insane." Thomas gasped.

"Perhaps I am. I certainly feel empty of everything. But just because I never loved you, don't assume that I wasn't fully aware of what I did."

"Thomas, be careful. She is hurting, she might be saying this to be to deliberately hurt–"

Carla had raised her arm and made a crushing motion with her hand. Hector clasped his hands to his throat and started to choke.

"Hector. Did you know there was always something I wanted to do after we split up?" She motioned with her arm towards the water. Hector fell to the floor with a loud slap. His body skidded along the jetty and flew off the end into the water. Carla lowered her hand and he sank several feet to the bottom of the lake. Bubbles of air broke the surface as he began to drown.

"Carla stop! What are you doing?" said Thomas, preparing to jump off the end of the jetty. Carla raised her other hand, and Thomas was frozen, mid stride.

"What do you care? Doesn't his presence anger you? Doesn't the image of us two writhing naked in bed together while you were hard at work, fill you with anger?"

"Let him go! Why are you being like this?" said Thomas staring out into the lake, unable to turn to look at her.

"Being like what? Did it ever occur to you that I was always like this? This is me. The way I always wanted to be."

"But killing people? Taking our daughter—"

"You know what? As I think back, that was probably the most fun part of it all!"

Thomas felt the rage surge through him. He forced his hand to raise and let the dense energy flow through him. He channeled it through his palms and red lightning forked from his hands towards Carla.

Carla leapt up with a surprising agility and leaped over them. She tumbled into a ball on the ground, near the house. Thomas aimed at Carla again. The lightning was so bright it was painful to watch.

Carla held her palm out towards the onslaught. It struck her hand and it was routed harmlessly to the ground.

Thomas intensified his attack, but the more he channeled his rage the more tired he became. Finally, Thomas dropped his arms. He felt drained from the release of such negative energy. His rage had evapourated. Thomas staggered backwards trying to catch his breath. Carla stood up and from her forehead she sent a powerful shockwave rippling towards Thomas. It shoved him square in the chest and threw him backwards through the air. He landed with a spine shuddering thump and skidded across the wooden jetty. His head banged into the wall of the house. As Thomas's head smacked against the solid wood, he lost consciousness.

Hector's lungs screamed at him, begging him to gasp for air. He watched helplessly as the last bubbles of air left his mouth and floated toward the surface. Each second seemed to pass like an eternity. Finally, his body betrayed him and he convulsed, taking a large gulp. His lungs filled with water. He convulsed and flailed against the lake bed, fighting the invisible force. Mud and silt clouded up around him. Each motion simply replaced the water in his lungs with fresh cold water. The light around him faded. Pain became a distant ache. Darkness grew around him and strange fluorescent shapes swam before his eyes.

He tried the only thing he had left, he tried to reach Carla's mind.

In the fleeting time between seconds, Hector burrowed deep into Carla's mind. The darkness inside her was suffocating.

Out of the black, terrifying creatures swam at him. Even through the gloom their many rows of teeth flashed menacingly from some unknown eerie light source. One swam by him, the wake of it sent him gamboling backwards.

He flailed and fought madly against the motion till he eventually regained control but he had no idea which way he was facing.

In every direction lay darkness. Another creature flashed by at the edge of his vision. He spun round and it was on him. The razor-sharp teeth bit into his flesh and he was catapulted out of Carla's mind. Back in his own dying brain he could hear Carla gloating.

You think you can control my mind, Hector?

It was worth a shot.

It's so disappointing, Hector. If only you hadn't left me.

That's rubbish! You never needed or even wanted me! You always wanted Thomas, that was why I left. I couldn't stand to be your dirty little secret when you had no intention of ever leaving him.

Well that may be true, but we still could have ruled this world together. With you I could have convinced the Council to support the Bactamrin years ago.
But what world would be left after you had finished selling all its inhabitants to the aliens for food?
It really doesn't matter Hector, if you won't work with me, I have no use for you. Now be a good boy and die quietly, and keep out of my mind!

Indecision

The doors to the council chamber burst open and out came the lead councilor.

"Yorik and Grace, please come in."

He led them back into the hall and down into the inner circle. The whole assembly watched the large squirrels hop down the stairs. At the bottom he offered them seats that had risen from the floor.

"Please, sit down."

The two squirrels and Eve sank down into the comfy padded chairs.

"We have come to a decision, pending a few questions if you will indulge us?"

"Of course, we want to help and it's only natural you have questions," Yorik said soothingly.

"We have voted to break our agreement with the Bactamrin and are very interested in your offer of help."

"Great," said Grace.

"Fantastic," agreed Yorik.

"But we have concerns, how do we know we can trust you? How do we know you aren't another species that will treat us in the same way the Bactamrin have?"

Yorik stood up. He lost his usual whimsical air and became quite serious as he addressed the many eyes upon them.

"In truth, you can't know. You will only find out if you choose to trust us," Yorik said, as he began to pace back and forth. "It's a leap of faith. All I can say is we will help you in any way we can, and we have much to teach you, if you want to listen."

There was a general murmur that rippled around the council.

"If it's any consolation we have been amongst you for several years now." Grace added. Yorik looked at her with a slightly exasperated look. If there were subtitles to it, they would have read "Really? And how is that possibly going to help them trust us?"

Grace read the expression, and the murmurs form the room.

"I just mean that we have been here, harming no-one and working to your benefit. Trust us, if we wanted to take your planet we could have done so easily by now." Grace further added, unhelpfully. Yorik slapped his paw across his face as the murmuring grew even more agitated.

"What Grace is trying to say, we have no interest in conquering another species or planet. There are more resources and planets out there for every life form to have its own home. That does not interest us. Saving your species however, does." said Yorik.

The assembly grew quiet again.

"There are many of us throughout every country and government. Do we seem like the Bactamrin? Have we taken any of your people? We are a peaceful species. A species that wants any other forms of life it encounters

to grow and flourish. That is why we are here. To save your species from one that nearly destroyed ours!"
There was a general murmur of approval amongst the crowd, some seemed comforted, but others were still disquieted at the thought of undercover aliens.
"Thank you, Grace and Yorik." He turned to address the room. "You have heard their answers. Please vote on whether we should accept help from the... erm-"
"The nearest pronunciation in your language would be Shilonoid," said Grace.
"The Sighlonoids' —"
"Close enough."
" — proposal of help. Unless anyone has any further questions?"
The room was silent.

Hector

Thomas opened his eyes, his head pounded to the beat of his heart. He saw Carla standing on the jetty with her eyes closed and her hands clenched by her sides. Thomas tried to stand up and instantly regretted it. His head swam, his vision blurred. Hecontinued to stand and took a swaying step towards her.

Carla heard him. She opened her eyes and launched another pressure wave at him. Thomas raised his arms above his head and crouched down. The wave crashed over him and dissipated harmlessly. Thomas lowered his arms and staggered back up.

He concentrated on forming a ball of electricity between his palms. A spinning ball of sparks formed and he threw it straight at her. Carla tried to shield herself from it but she was distracted fighting Hector in the mental realm, it hit her squarely in the chest. The energy discharged all over her body twisting her muscles in spasms and forcing them to contort uncontrollably. She fell to the floor.

Thomas stumbled over to her and checked for a pulse. It was rapid, but strong. He raced down to the end of the jetty and peered into the water. He saw Hector's lifeless body resting on the bottom of the lake bed. Thomas reached into the water and tried to grab him. "Forget it, he's dead." Carla groaned from behind him.

Decision

After the councilors had shuffled back into the hall, fresh from their comfort breaks, the lead Councillor stood once more in the center of the room.

"Councilors, I can now reveal the result of the vote. For the order of business: should we permit the Shiholinoids to stay on our planet and assist us." He took a breath for added effect.

"The result is," another overly dramatic pause, "For: six hundred and sixty-eight. Against: two hundred and twenty-four. The motion is carried."

A cheer went up around the room releasing a great deal of pressure. Grace and Yorik knew the majority were terrified of fighting the Bactamrin alone. They were grateful for any form of help.

"Please accept this as an offer of welcome and friendship from our planet to yours," he said, turning to Grace and Yorik. Yorik stood and hopped over to the spot light.

"Thank you, but I fear all too soon you will be needing us more than you realise. As a symbol of our goodwill we have prepared a shielding system for the planet." The crowd gasped.

"You see, we always wanted to protect you. Now however, as you have trusted us, we will trust you. We will, with your agreement, start working with you to create weapons and ships that would be greatly advanced compared to your present ones. Together we will create a fleet and when our home ships reach this solar system, we will attack them from both sides! Together we will defeat them! We will eradicate them, so they never threaten another species again!"

The councilors cheered and applauded. Some stood and vocalised their excitement. Yorik and Grace looked up at the assembly and smiled. It was heart-warming, but inside they feared for mankind. The humans had barely tasted the devastation and terrifying might of the Bactamrin. Something they would soon learn once the agreement with them had been broken.

Grace looked at the excited crowd, they had hope again. But then something niggled at her, something that started when Yorik had mentioned eradicating them. She realised she was feeling empathy for the Bactamrin! Despite their particular cuisine choices, they were just a species trying to survive too. They weren't attacking Earth because of any bad feeling or motive, it was simply the next food supply. She couldn't help feeling like she was watching a theater of hope, powered by a common fear. Was this the answer? Was the only way to stop the Bactamrin to fight it?

Alas, Poor Hector

Thomas looked around and saw that Carla had teleported to sit perched on the edge of the roof. She held her head with her right hand.

"Why the hell would you want to kill him?" Thomas cried and jumped into the water. He grabbed Hector and pulled him to the surface. As he dragged him up onto the jetty, he heard Carla's cold laugh behind him. Thomas checked Hector for any signs of life but there were none.

"Can't you help him?" Thomas pleaded.

"I could. But I won't."

"What is wrong with you Carla?"

"Be grateful I have stopped pummeling you with air waves."

"Let me guess, it's just another game? You're going to let me save him and then kill us both?"

"That would be amusing, but no. Hector is dead. You however, I haven't decided what I will do with just yet. It would be a waste to kill you. Besides, Eve would never forgive me."

Thomas started hitting Hector's chest. He wasn't really sure what he was doing but he had seen a robot doctor do it in the hospital once. Carla started laughing again. Thomas opened Hector's eyes trying to see a reaction to the light, but they were empty and lifeless. Carla's mirth from the situation angered him. He spun round and fired another, stronger lightning ball at Carla.

Carla clicked her fingers and she was transported back down onto the jetty, a couple of feet from Thomas. The ball of lightning continued sailing into the sky.
"Really? Still trying?" she goaded.
Carla felt a small prickling sensation in her mind. She looked down at Hector's lifeless body. Somehow, he had broken through her defenses and he was poking around in her mind. She scoured her mental realm for signs of him, but he was well hidden.
Hector was deep inside Carla's mind but he knew his time there was short. His body was practically dead. Everything was turning numb and he felt a coldness creeping across him. Carla's ego and mirth had let the slightest of small cracks appear in her mental defenses. Hector jumped at the chance to dive into her mind and was now working his way to her emotion center. If he could gain control of her body for a few minutes, he might be able to bring his body back to life. At the very least he was determined to buy some time for Thomas. He probed her conscious thoughts and was hit by waves of hatred, pain, and loss.
Hector felt the slender tendrils that linked him back to his own body begin to fade. He was nearly out of time. He would soon lose all connection with his body and drift away. He decided to make a last thrust into her brain before he lost himself completely. Hector projected into her mind the most distracting, annoying thing he could think of.

Carla felt an eerie sensation creeping up her spine. It spread out all over her skin. She felt it tingle, then prickle. Suddenly she needed to scratch. Everywhere on her body felt itchy. At first it felt like ants were crawling over her. Then the ants started to bite. As she scratched more and more furiously it felt like the bites had become swollen and infected. Her skin was on fire. She sank to the ground clawing at herself and started to wail in pain.

Thomas saw her battling the mind attack and grabbed the opportunity. He mustered every bit of energy he had left, every part of his will to live and survive. Thomas sent a single piercing bolt of electricity towards Carla. It hit her and lifted her into the air. Her body, wrapped in sparks, flew off the side of the jetty. She hit the water some distance from the edge and sank like a stone. Thomas felt completely drained as he turned back to Hector.

"Hector," he said.

Thomas! He heard Hector's voice inside his head.

"Hector! Are you okay? We'll get you to the hospital! STAY WITH US!"

It's too late Thomas, my body has died.

"You've got to hold on Hector, we'll get you to the squirrels, they will know what to do!"

I don't think even they can help with this Thomas.

Thomas felt an uncomfortable lump forming in his throat.

I'm actually feeling quite at peace Thomas, thank you.

"I practically got you killed!"

No, don't feel bad for that. You gave me a wonderful ending. One last adventure, it was quite something. I could never have lived for long without Sara. I felt my life empty the moment her eyes closed for the last time. Now I get to join her.

"Hector- I'm so sorry, I can't believe—"

Don't be upset Thomas, this is a good thing for me. I'm just starting another adventure.

"It's just that we, I mean it was a laugh—" Thomas swallowed and rolled his eyes, desperate to stop even one tear from forming.

This connection is getting harder to keep up with, so I have to go Thomas.

Thomas nodded, a tear finally escaping his futile grip on his emotions. Thomas's mind went deathly quiet. Only the thumping of his heart pierced the silence. it could only mean that Hector had gone. He couldn't quite believe it. Although he had only known Hector a few days, he felt they had become friends. He knew there was something about him that he would miss forever. A tear broke free from the brave grip of his resolve and fell onto the warped wood of the jetty.

Into the breach

During the following years the Council broke their agreement with the Bactamrin. War broke out almost instantly and the human species was pushed to near the edge of extinction. With only the Shilonoid's to protect them the Bactamrin continually attacked and plundered the planet. However, with the same spirit that has kept the human species alive for centuries, it fought back. Eventually the raids started to decrease, as new tactics and warfare methods were contrived. One area that luckily survived the worst of the raids was Lana. Apparently not even human eating aliens were particularly fond of that town.

Thomas watched the ginormous metallic grey transport ship rise above the treeline on the distant hill behind his house. It floated unnaturally upwards into the dark heavy clouds. Another supply ship leaving from the old Preparation Station on its way to the new space stations that were hastily building warships. With the cloaking shields now removed from the cities and other technologically advanced areas, the spaceports traffic could easily be seen by everyone, even from Lana.

He walked back up the jetty and into his house. Inside Eve was making the last preparations and additions to her luggage. It amazed him how much she had grown these last years. Not just in height, but in power.

The council and squirrels had trained her in all manner of mental abilities. She could teleport, control minds, communicate telepathically, and create illusions that would have fooled Carla. Sometimes she scared him a little. But then she'd smile at him and he would see the innocent bright girl he knew so well. Her kind heart and wise mind made him glow inside.

Eve was staying whilst on holiday before she had to travel to the central space station. Grace and Yorik were already up there reinforcing the satellite array that protected the Earth from the Bactamrin.

"All ready?" asked Thomas.

"I think so," she said with a touch of sadness. She tilted her beautiful head to the side. "Dad, are you sure you're going to be alright? You don't want to come with me?"

"I'll cope. It's not like I don't have good company to help me through," he said, waving towards the armchair where her grandfather Wilf snoozed. He gave a timely snort as if in agreement.

Eve threw her arms around him and kissed his cheek. "I'll really miss you."

"It won't be the same around here without you."

They released each other and Eve wiped away a tear forming in her eye.

"Why won't you come with me? You know they are desperate for people with your talents."

"I know, but I've had enough of that to fill a lifetime."

"But you don't have to fight. You could train people like I do."

"Maybe someday Eve. But right now I like being here. Close to home, close to Gaia. It feels like I should be here right now."

"Ok, but you can't spend your life in this dusty house feeling sorry for yourself!"

"I know, and it's not just that, it's—"

"It's okay Dad, I get it," interrupted Eve. Even though she had promised never to look into his mind, she couldn't resist. Inside he was a swirling mess of emotions and underneath it all he was just tired of life. Tired of the pain in losing people, tired of the bureaucracy and fighting to get sensible ideas heard. The few years he had spent working with the Council after that day had exhausted him. He had fought so hard to stop the bickering and to concentrate on building the defenses they needed. They had drained his spirit. But not before he had first helped form alliances that were fundamental to the building of the space stations. She knew what really lay inside him. Quietly smoldering beneath the tiredness was the passion to keep fighting, the will to make this a better place and drive people back together. Whenever she peered into his mind, she always injected a spark of excitement and determination. She knew it would be a few short months before he would be joining her on the station.

Space Station Zeus

Approximately twenty-two thousand miles above their heads, two giant squirrels were floating in the control room of an orbiting satellite. It was a lumbering metal box about the size of a large bus with several long solar panels extending into the inky black space either side of it. The room they were in had no windows, only doors above and below them that led to the other two chambers. Yorik floated weightlessly above the main laser array panel and was shouting at Grace. Grace was braced against a metal cabinet that contained a huge amount of flashing lights. Most were green, but there were some angry red ones that flashed at her menacingly.

"WELL SWITCH IT OVER THEN," yelled Yorik.
"ALRIGHT! ALRIGHT," Grace screamed back.
"Ready? Shifting projection bank three into phase alignment."
"Okay."
"Done!"

Several of the flashing lights went out, then flickered to green. There was just one remaining red light, but it was the biggest and the angriest.

"Fusion containment field Alpha, still partial," said Grace.
"What? Well reboot it!"
"Ok, three, two, one." Grace flipped a big switch and the whole satellite was plunged into darkness.

"YOU STUPID GIT! THAT WAS THE MAIN GRID! GET IT BACK ON, NOW!"

"OKAY, OKAY!!"

The power flickered back on but the red light returned. Grace pointed at it. "It's still knackered." she added.

"I know, I know. Plug the bypass into socket three nine two."

"Okay." Grace grabbed at one of the loose floating cables and rammed it into a socket in front of her.

"Ready? I'm just going to send it a resynch. In three, two, one." Yorik tapped a small section of the control panel. A large spark arced through the cable and struck Grace. She was thrown across the room and hit the opposite side with a splat.

The lights dimmed, then flickered back to normal, the light went green.

"Hey we did it!"

Grace floated slowly spinning back across the room, her eyes were wide and dazed and her fur was smoldering. It looked cartoonishly surreal to see a large squirrel drifting across the control room leaving a little smoke trail.

"Grace," Yorik yelled. It startled her and she seemed to regain her focus.

"WHAT THE BLOODY HELL WAS THAT?"

"Hey! I didn't know that would happen, did I?" Yorik said, hiding his smirk.

"So, what now?"

"Well, that's it. This last one is now online! Should help hold them for another couple of years at least. Ready to head back?"

"Yeah," said Grace, patting down her smoldering fur. They vanished from the control room and almost instantly popped back into existence in the docking bay of space station Zeus. It was the core station that contained the administration and logistical units of Earth's new army. It was also rapidly turning into the main training center for their Psych Warriors, as they were now colloquially called.

The docking bay was buzzing with activity as various ships arrived and departed. Hundreds of people scurried around the deck controlling the various machines that serviced the spacecraft. Yorik and Grace scampered across the great floor and headed into the lobby at the far end. They took one of the many lifts up several floors and entered the meeting room complex. In the plush, brightly lit corridors they moved swiftly and took the first doorway that led to an empty room. Once inside Yorik sent a mental call out to all their operatives. It was calling for a meeting.

Yorik created a virtual space in his mind and opened it for any Shilonoid to enter. The room he created was from one of his favourite memories from human history, an old cathedral. The walls rose high on either side and vanished into a mist that hung above them. The figure of a large grey squirrel with patches of black fur popped into existence in the center of the room.

"Yorik," the squirrel called.

"William, prompt as ever, good to see you."

Grace popped into the space just to the left of Yorik. One by one, the room filled up with large squirrels of various colours and patterns. Eventually, when the room had filled, Yorik stood on a small pedestal he had just imagined into existence.

"Thank you for your time on such short notice. Grace and I have just completed the upgrades to the shield array. They are now online and should keep the humans safe for a few years. How are we progressing on building the ships for them, Selma?"

A red squirrel, halfway down the hall squeaked. Yorik projected another pedestal under the squirrel's feet and she was lifted above the others.

"The construction is going to plan. They have taken to our new technologies rather well. In fact, we could be producing numbers well above the targets by the end of the year."

"Good, fantastic work, Selma. Edward, how is our fleet fairing?"

Selma sank back into the crowd and as another red squirrel started to speak, he rose into the air.

"After the engine rebuilds, the time has been cut considerably. We're around twenty-five Earth years away. We are approaching another rift but we've enhanced our shields and with the extra capacity we'll pass through easily this time."

"Brilliant. Herella, what about the Bactamrin?"

This time a large grey squirrel rose above the rest. "They have established a significant base on Mars. It looks like they are mining for resources but have found little to help them so far. Their raids on Earth are still intense but the frequency is dropping. We are still losing pilots, ships, and innocents."

"Thank you, Herella. Are the raids concentrated in one area?"

"It seems random, but the points they center on are areas with large populations. We suspect they are running low on resources and taking the easiest targets they can."

"Thanks, Herella. Let us know if they make any progress on their mining. The last thing we need is for them to gain another foothold in this system. Terrence, what are the battle plans looking like?"

"We are still heavily outnumbered, even with the projections of what the human fleet can be built up to. However, the humans are learning mental abilities and skills quicker than we thought they would. Eve will be joining us shortly and we're excited about her potential. She is young but is already so powerful and talented. We have no doubt she will accelerate the training program."

"And Carla? Can we trust her? Has anyone worked out what happened to her yet?"

"I think so, she seems permanently changed. She's doing a fine job with the psychic training program.

Some of the new trainees are already showing powerful skills."

"Enough to match the Bactamrin?"

"Possibly, I think so, yes. Although they are still very inexperienced in battle."

"When our ships are nearer it may be worth starting to conduct some raids of our own; to help train them in real combat."

"A great idea."

"Right, well if that's all the updates. Does anyone have any other issues they wish to mention?"

The room was silent.

"Great, thank you all again. We'll meet next month back in the usual time and place."

The squirrels began to vanish from the hall. When the last had left, Grace and Yorik drifted back to the reality of the room aboard the space station.

They left the room and headed back to the lifts. As the doors slid open, they saw a young female face in front of them.

"Grace! Yorik!" Eve cried as she rushed out to hug them.

Yorik and Grace had become quite fond of Eve and showed a rare flash of elation at seeing her again.

"Eve!"

"How have you both been? Finished the upgrades then?"

"Yeah, we just finished."

"Great, then you can buy me lunch and tell me about yourselves. It must have been at least a year since I last saw you?"

Yorik was about to make their excuses but caught the look in Eve's eye. He loved the way she was so full of life and hope, it was infectious. She had a spirit that made any doubts he had of the human race surviving vanish into thin air.

They traveled up the many floors to the nearest food hall. In the large bustling room, they collected their food and found a table. They were fortunate in that the last shift had yet to finish. The place was relatively empty so they managed to get one of the coveted window tables that looked out over the blue pearl of Earth.

As they sat and chatted about all the events of the last year, Grace and Yorik quizzed her about how Thomas was getting on. Eve was fascinated by the war and the preparations the Shilonoids were busy with. An alarm rang out marking the end of the shift and soon the place began to fill up with soldiers, labourers, and teachers. Eve saw a familiar face that she was surprisingly looking forward to talking to again, it was Carla.

"So, are you ever going to tell Thomas?" Eve asked the squirrels.

"About Carla? Eventually maybe. I think once Thomas has decided to re-join us, he'll understand. If we told him now, he would never come back," replied Grace.

"And the other thing about Carla?"
"The other thing? You mean how she actually survived?"
"No, I mean about how she is—" Eve looked at the confused faces and realised. "You don't actually know do you?"
"Know what? We have been observing Carla closely but, apart from the shift in her personality, she seems perfectly fine."
Carla had seen them and made her way across the room. A few paces from their table she seemed to have a crisis of confidence and hesitated.
"Carla! Come and join us," Eve beamed, sensing her awkwardness.
"Hi Eve, Grace, Yorik," she said, gingerly setting her tray down and pulling up a chair.
"Carla relax! We're way beyond what happened now. It was years ago! Why are you still so nervous anyway?"
"I dunno," she said staring out towards Earth. "Sometimes something dark comes over me and I doubt my own thoughts. It's quite peculiar, like someone else has control over my mind for a fleeting second. But it passes quickly. It just leaves me feeling a bit unsure of myself."
Eve reached out the tendrils of her mind and connected with Carla. She had practiced this so much she had it down to a fine art, in seconds they were communicating telepathically.

Eve, how's your dad?
Better, but still the same. When are you going to tell him?
Do you think he's ready?
Maybe, but I don't know how he'll take it, he may hate you but he's still mourning you. Why don't you just tell him and get it over with?
If I did tell him, even after the shock of finding out that I'm not dead, he certainly wouldn't believe that I've changed. The only way he'd believe it is by seeing what I'm like now, over time. Even then he's always going to be suspicious of me.
You're right Carla, let's wait till he comes to us.
He's coming?
Not straight away, but the squirrels believe he will be soon. I think they're right. You know how he is, can't stay out of things for long.
You're probably right, Eve. By the way, the whole station is abuzz with your arrival! I hear that you have become quite the Psy Warrior, probably the most powerful we have!
Really? Thanks Carla, or are you Hector today?

About The Author

Darren Ashworth is a writer from the heart of England, the Midlands. Where people are friendly and kind spirited.

He spent his years bouncing from jobs such as butchery to packing fishing tackle and eventually found his way into computing. He managed to carve out a moderately successful career writing computer programs for clients who turned out not to need them anyway.

Through all of his mortgage paying years, the passion to write and create his own worlds has always remained.

These Times is his first bold step into doing what he believes he was put on the earth to do.